MEET CUTE

LOVE, CAMERA, ACTION #5

ELISE FABER

MEET CUTE
BY ELISE FABER

This is a work of fiction. Names, places, characters, and events are fictitious in every regard. Any similarities to actual events and persons, living or dead, are purely coincidental. Any trademarks, service marks, product names, or named features are assumed to be the property of their respective owners and are used only for reference. There is no implied endorsement if any of these terms are used. Except for review purposes, the reproduction of this book in whole or part, electronically or mechanically, constitutes a copyright violation.

LOVE, CAMERA, ACTION

CHAPTER ONE

Talbot

I LISTENED to the sounds of the party on the other side of the hedges, and I knew I should be out there, schmoozing and charming and making sure everyone was happy and having a great time.

This had been my idea, after all.

To surprise my friend, Maggie, and her fiancé, Aaron, with an engagement party after their return from Italy where Aaron had popped the question.

I'd helped Aaron pick the ring, run through the words he was going to say as though he were a fellow actor and I was helping him prep for a scene.

Then I'd helped Maggie do the same.

Because my friend knew what she wanted and needed, and that wasn't waiting for her man to propose.

If she wanted to get married, she had no problem doing the asking.

And in the race down the aisle, Mags had won.

Not that it was a surprise. She was the smartest, most beautiful, most *alive* person I'd ever met.

If only there'd been a spark between us.

But that was the problem.

I didn't feel sparks. I didn't feel much of *anything*. I poured everything I had onto the screen. I worked until every emotion in me was gone . . . and then when they came back, I did it all over again. And again.

And again.

But even giving everything I could, the itchy sensation never went away.

I was FOMO-ing. I was missing out on something *more*.

But what?

I'd climbed from obscurity to leading roles. Most even with great scripts . . . or at least feel-good, fun storylines that were a blast to make. I had several houses and cars. I was the face of multiple products, including a delicious Chardonnay produced by none other than Aaron's winery.

What could I possibly want or need or be missing out on?

A woman.

Unfortunately, as much as I tried to pretend that *wasn't* the issue, deep down, it was at the crux of everything. I had friends, *good* friends, but it wasn't the same. I wanted what Mags had, what my other friends Artie, Pierce, and Eden had.

Which was . . . more.

Which was . . . *everything*.

But it was elusive, that *everything*, especially when I couldn't walk down the street without being photographed, when I couldn't be certain that someone in the business who wanted to date me wasn't using me to move up, or worse, would sell me out to the tabloids.

I was one of the most successful men in the world . . . and I was lonely.

Sighing, I pushed off the tree I'd been leaning against —*hiding behind*—and knew this wasn't a problem I could fix tonight. I needed to leave my safe little enclave and put myself back out there, to make sure my friends had the wonderful party they deserved.

Even though I'd given myself the mental pep talk, I hadn't so much as taken a step toward the exit, when a woman walked in.

Or rather, limped in.

She walked right over to the tree I was leaning against, the one planted in the center of this walled and sheltered garden, and placed a palm against it, using her free hand to yank off her heels. "Ow," she muttered, chucking one at the hedges. "Fucking heels." She tore off the other. "Stupid, fucking death traps." That heel sailed through the air, bouncing off the leaves and landing with impressive accuracy near its partner. Then she started lifting the edge of her skirt, muttering about "Stupid pantyhose," and I realized my mistake.

I should have announced my presence *before* the disrobing began.

I should at least do it *now*.

But I found myself frozen, arrested by the golden skin revealed as she peeled down the stockings inch by inch, the glimpse of black lace when the hem of her skirt slid the wrong —or rather, the *right*, in my opinion—way.

Curves I could hold on to. Softly gilded skin. Ass. Hips. Breasts. Face. They were all incredible, but it was her legs that made my mouth go dry with the need to trace my tongue over. Every. Single. Inch.

In fact, I was so focused on the sight of her legs that I missed her arm moving behind her, missed the fact that one of those shapely thighs had a black holster strapped around it, that her luscious curves hid a gun.

A gun that was now pointed in my direction with rock-steady hands.

"Who the fuck are you?" she snapped.

CHAPTER TWO

Tammy

MY HANDS DIDN'T SHAKE as I pointed the gun at the most handsome man I'd ever laid eyes on.

I was too well trained for them to shake.

But I did feel a curl of heat lick through my abdomen, dip lower to trail between my thighs.

"Easy," he said, his striking gold eyes meeting mine, his hands up, palms facing toward me.

Big hands.

Big . . .

I blinked. "Who are you?" I asked again.

"I'm Talbot."

Shit. *Shit.*

"As in Maggie's boss, Talbot?"

A nod. "As in Maggie's *friend*, Talbot."

Triple shit.

I lowered the gun, quickly re-holstered it, smoothing the skirt of my dress down. I hated the heels and pantyhose—or rather thigh-highs, because I wasn't sure anyone actually wore pantyhose any longer. Maggie, whom I'd borrowed the set from (because thigh-chafing was a real thing, yo), certainly hadn't had any. But I still should have been more aware of my surroundings before I'd started chucking belongings and stripping down.

Fucking hell.

I wasn't normally so . . . cranky? (no, I was definitely cranky), unaware? (that was true, as a police officer, I had been trained to always have a baseline of my surroundings), off my mark (*that* was it).

Capable would be the word in the dictionary under my name.

Right along with normal, cute, and boring.

Which was what had brought me into hiding.

Out there . . . was Hollywood.

And I was me. I was a normal woman from a small town, who had a normal job and wasn't used to schmoozing with celebrities.

Not that any of them had been mean or treated me like I didn't belong. In fact, they'd all been really nice. And even though I'd been expecting a lot of industry talk, plenty of inside jokes or conversations where I had no clue what they were about, that hadn't been my experience. All the pretty people Maggie hung out with were also all nice people.

And I was still me.

Not particularly nice.

Not particularly pretty—at least not when compared to Hollywood standards. When I looked in the mirror, however, I shrugged and thought *not too bad*. Hazel eyes that changed depending on what I wore, transforming from brown to gold to green, sometimes even to gray. Blond hair that was shoulder length, but that I most often wrestled back into a ponytail because I couldn't stand the flyaways in my face. A strong body, in a normal (an eight, sometimes even a ten or twelve, depending on the brand) size. I was fine. I didn't hate myself, didn't despise the image in the mirror.

It was just . . . when I stood next to the rest of them in all their gorgeousness . . .

Yeah, it was a bit of hell on the self-confidence.

Doubly so because I was more comfortable in jeans and T-shirts. Certainly more comfortable in them than in fancy cocktail dresses and high heels.

And pantyhose.

Or thigh-highs to prevent chafing, because unlike some of the women out there, my thighs touched. Go me.

"So, you going to tell me why you're in the habit of pulling guns on innocent men?"

I yanked my brain back to reality, focused on the man in front of me.

"Um, last time I checked, peeping Toms were doing illegal shit."

A brow lifted. "But am I really a peeping Tom if a woman starts stripping down in front of me?"

His tone was light, but I detected an undertone.

"Oh, my God."

The other brow joined the first. "What?"

"*Have* women stripped down in front of you?"

He rested one broad shoulder against the tree trunk. "For a role or in real life?"

"That you have to make that clarification concerns me considerably," I muttered, moving toward the hedge and scooping up my heels. "If I had to hazard a guess, I'd say I wasn't the first woman to strip in front of you—both for a role and in real life."

His laughter was like warm honey.

Literally.

I actually felt it coat my skin, skate over my body, dripping down until it made its way to where those thigh-highs had stopped, where my holster was now situated.

Aw hell.

"You'd be right," he said, pushing up and crossing toward me. "Though, only one of those was welcome."

"I can guess which one."

His eyes, sparkling pools of gold danced as they met mine. "I'd bet you'd guess wrong."

Yeah. Sure. Like any guy I knew wouldn't welcome a woman stripping down in front of him. That would be a freaking dream for any man I'd ever known—and I'd known a lot, since my job was male-dominated.

But then Talbot proved that he wasn't like any man I knew.

And maybe, I fell for him, just a little bit.

Like in the way a teenager fantasized about a celebrity, imagining how it would feel to meet them, to kiss and hold them, even knowing that the reality of that would never actually come true.

Although, in my reality, when he touched me, it wasn't just in my head.

CHAPTER THREE

Talbot

I HALF-EXPECTED the gun to make a reappearance when I knelt at her feet.

But instead her lips—lush enough to have a man (*cough, me*) consider all the different ways to sip at that mouth, to taste every millimeter—parted, a breath sliding out.

"What are you doing?" she whispered.

I took the heels from her, held the first one out so she could step into it.

"What is this?" she asked again, those lips pressing flat, suspicion drifting into her pretty hazel eyes.

"I'm trying to help."

Her gaze held mine, and a thread of derision crept in. "Is there a secret camera around? Someone who's going to jump out and say, 'Gotcha!' and laugh at the small-town hick who's playing *Cinderella* with the movie star?"

I kept my hands—and the shoes—where they were. "Nope."

She rolled her eyes. "Nope? That's it?"

"Yup." I waved the heel. "You need to put these back on, don't you?"

Her face scrunched up in a way that was totally adorable, and I felt my heart actually skip a beat. God, she was so fucking cute. Especially when she grumbled, "Maybe, but I don't really want to."

I chuckled. "Come on . . ." I paused.

"You just realized you don't know Cinderella's real name, didn't you?"

Of course, I had just realized that. Because I was a dumbass who hadn't asked. This woman knew me because she knew Maggie, knew I was her boss . . . but that right there was a clue, wasn't it?

Normally, I'd have my assistant put together a guest list, arrange all the details.

But I'd handled this one myself—including sending all the invites *and* hand-addressing them, thank me very much. Which meant, I just needed to use my awesome short-term memory— who ever said actors didn't have *some* handy real-world skills? —to deduce this woman's name.

Not from town. One glance had told me that much.

She didn't have that hungry expression of someone in the industry, and she was far too into simple, real beauty to be from Southern California. Light makeup, unstyled hair, an unassuming dress, heels from a common big box store.

Not that I was judging her.

She looked absolutely beautiful, completely appealing, much more so than any of the women I'd laid eyes on in the last few months. Hell, maybe the last few years.

It was just . . . context as I searched my mental database for names.

Blond. Not from town. Maggie's friend.

She could only be one person.

"Oh, no," I said, lightly gripping her ankle and bringing her foot up. She wavered, and her hands went to my shoulders, just as I'd planned—*muhaha*—and I slid the heel onto a foot with sky blue painted toenails. "I know who you are. You're Tammy, and you're from Darlington."

Maggie's tiny hometown in Northeastern Utah.

I kept scrounging those memory banks when Tammy's lips parted, her eyes widening in surprise. "You're a police officer," I said. "Which explains the gun." I tapped a finger to my chin. "Though I'm not sure you're abiding by California's concealed carry permit restrictions. The gun laws here are pretty strict."

A roll of those hazel eyes, and I was caught for a moment as they seemed to shift from tawny brown to a streaked emerald.

They really were the most gorgeous pair of eyes I'd ever seen.

"Well, technically, as an enforcement officer, federal law allows me to carry across the country," she said, mock-condescension in her tone, "so don't you worry your pretty little head."

I wanted to worry about her.

That urge came on hot and heavy and intense. This yearning to be something to this woman, to understand the emotions flickering across her face, to mean something to her, even though, by rights, we'd only met a bare five minutes before.

Bare.

Heh.

I recognized the burst of humor for what it was.

Reality pushing fantasy away. Because as much as Tammy might be fascinating and beautiful and a little distant when everyone else around me always seemed to want to get closer, as much as that trifecta was absolutely intoxicating, our worlds were too far apart.

She'd go home and back to her life.

I'd move on with mine.

"Lean on me," I told her.

Her fingers clenched my shoulders, and I felt an arrow of desire fly straight toward my cock.

If she were a normal woman of my sphere, if she weren't Mags' friend, I'd turn on the charm, I'd beg, borrow, and steal to get Tammy into my bed.

But Mags *was* my friend and my publicist.

And I, for lack of a better and less crass phrase, I didn't shit where I ate.

"Come on," I coaxed, sliding my hand up the calf above her bare foot, feeling silken skin under my palm and determinedly ignoring the way my cock twitched. *Mags' friend. Mags' friend. Mags'*—

She teetered, gripping tighter, her weight moving forward and her thighs brushing against my face.

"I'm sorry," she said, immediately putting distance between us.

"No worries." I slipped the other shoe on when she lifted her foot, resisting the urge to shift my hand higher, kicking myself for *playing Cinderella,* as she'd called it.

The hint of her against my nose, knowing there was black lace beneath, adding my hand on her bare skin and having caught a glimpse of those luscious thighs as she'd peeled the stocking down one inch at a time . . . yeah, none of that was great for my self-control, nor for the whole *Mags' friend* thing.

Good times.

I set her foot down, forced my hands to drop away from her skin, and stood.

"Thanks," she murmured.

"You're welcome." And then I stood there like a dope.

My only consolation was that she was standing there like a dope just like me. For my part, I was transfixed as the twinkling strands of bulbs hanging over the garden flashed across her face, transforming the colors of her eyes like the most intoxicating light show.

She . . . I didn't know her well enough to say for sure.

But I did feel the heavy weight of her gaze on my body,

tracing down and back up, as though her fingers were stroking across my chest, my torso . . . *lower.*

I don't know who shifted closer—if it was me who'd taken the first step or her—but suddenly I found my chest against hers, my fingers brushing along the outside of her arm.

My voice was a murmur. "Are you—"

A mistake. Speaking right then. I should have continued with the stroking, kept on with the brushing, the moving closer, then maybe . . .

She straightened, taking a huge step back, kept retreating as she pointed a finger at my chest. "Next time, if a woman starts disrobing, thinking she's in private, you need to speak up." Eyes narrowing. "Before she takes off her clothes."

I bit back a smile. "One might say that a woman who's disrobing, thinking she's in private, should, perhaps, confirm that she is in private."

Thunderclouds sailed through those eyes.

But she didn't snap back as I'd half-expected.

As—I might as well be honest—I'd half-hoped.

She was gorgeous just standing there as she was, but she was absolutely beautiful while pointing a gun at me like some deadly assassin. I could see the camera angles, picture the shots. If a director could capture that fierceness in her expression and deliver it on screen, it would be a hit.

Especially when it was juxtaposed with this.

The girl next door.

Except, I didn't want to share her with the world. I didn't want her face on the big screen or in millions of homes. And suddenly, I thought, to hell with the fact that she was Mags' friend, screw that she lived several states away.

I wanted her for *me.*

My feet carried me to her. "Tammy—"

The *tink, tink, tink* of someone tapping a glass invaded the space, the voices outside the garden quieting, until just one rose above all else.

Maggie's.

"Thank you all for coming tonight," she said.

Tammy stiffened, slanted one more glance in my direction, before darting from the garden, leaving me with the urge to chase her down, to clock her over the head, and drag her back to my home, caveman style.

I didn't, obviously.

Because one, I wasn't a caveman and I'd never been with a woman who'd not wanted me, let alone chased one down who was clearly trying to escape my presence.

And two, because Maggie kept talking.

"But I wanted to extend the biggest thank you to the man who brought Aaron and me together, who was instrumental in our dueling engagement plots—" The crowd laughed here, and I knew I needed to get out there, knew that she would be saying my name. I headed for the exit then stopped.

Because . . . the stockings.

Probably, I should have left them.

But some perverse part of me wanted to touch the silk that had encased those sexy legs.

"My boss, my best friend, and one of the greatest people in all the world . . ."

I snatched them up, darted out of the garden, just in time for Maggie to say, "Talbot!"

Her eyes found mine, joy in their depths, and then she came to me, hugging me tight, her lips to my ear. "Thank you, Tal," she murmured. "Thank you for everything."

Light applause greeted her words, and I hugged her back. "You deserve every moment of it." Then I released her and told the crowd, "Let's all have a drink for the future bride and groom's happy marriage."

Louder applause this time.

She nudged my shoulder.

"You always do know how to play the crowd."

I kissed the top of her head, surreptitiously glancing around for Tammy. She was in a circle of conversation, just a few feet away from us, and glaring at me.

Which made me smile.

Her lips flattened further. But her eyes . . . in those pretty hazel eyes there was *heat*.

Oh yes, I needed to find a way to make this woman mine.

CHAPTER FOUR

Tammy

I COULD HAVE STAYED in the small cottage on the back of Artie and Pierce's property where the party had been held. They'd offered.

Yup, freaking *movie* stars had offered.

But I'd declined, even though Maggie had already moved out.

She'd been staying to save up money to buy a place in the expensive Los Angeles real estate market, but considering she was going to marry Aaron—who co-owned a series of successful wineries located all over the world, each with a house for them to use on property, Mags hadn't needed the space.

So now she had a nest egg *and* houses around the world.

Who could complain?

Certainly, not my blissfully happy childhood friend. The same friend who'd left our small town and built a successful life for herself. We'd only just begun to reconnect, and I was glad for it—and not because of the Hollywood connection. Maggie was a good person, and I hadn't had too many good people in my life.

It was nice to add another.

Still, none of that, Hollywood or good people or tempting digs or otherwise, were why I wasn't staying in the guest house.

Nope.

This was my first time visiting L.A. The first time I'd been to California.

So, I was making the most of it.

I had all of the tourist sites planned out, starting with a trip to *The Happiest Place on Earth* in the morning. Yup, I was hitting the amusement park, and I was going to gorge myself on churros and popcorn and soft pretzels and ice cream. I was going to pay exorbitant amounts of money for souvenirs and had already purchased an entrance ticket that cost in the realm of what I'd spent on my first car. I was set, and the best part?

My hotel was right across the street.

I couldn't wait to spend the entire day walking around and seeing the sights and experiencing every attraction until my feet felt ready to fall off. And then, only then, would I go back to my hotel room and collapse into bed.

I couldn't *freaking* wait.

But first, I needed to get to my car.

I found Maggie, gave her a quick hug, during which she reminded me of my upcoming dinner three nights from then.

"I'm so glad you came," she said, holding my hands tight after I'd promised I would be there.

"I needed the vacation," I told her. "This gave me the perfect excuse." I lightly squeezed her hands. "I'm so happy for you both. I'm glad you found your way back to each other."

Mags hadn't just left Darlington when she'd gone out to chase her dreams. She'd left the boy who loved her. She'd left Aaron.

And that road back to each other hadn't been the least bit easy.

"Thanks," she whispered.

"I'll see you in a few days," I whispered back.

I waved to Aaron, picked up my purse and coat from the bag check area, and then meandered my way down the long driveway filled with cars. My feet absolutely ached, and my legs were chilly, sans stockings—which I just remembered I'd left in the garden.

For a moment, I debated going back and retrieving them.

But then I'd need to weave back through the guests and potentially have to explain why I'd taken them off in the first place, and that would make for an awkward conversation—

Which wasn't why I was avoiding going back.

Nope. That had to do with putting as much distance between myself and one Talbot Green.

The man with the golden eyes was dangerous to my psyche.

He made those fantasies want to be real.

And that was the real fantasy, because they never would be.

With that lovely, cynical thought, I shrugged into my coat, pulled the keys to my rental out, and continued walking. I'd parked outside the gate, a long way down the road. The guest list was quite extensive, and I hadn't dared to navigate my way through the Bentleys and Range Rovers.

Also, yay for a long walk in these freaking heels.

I should have packed sneakers in my purse. That would have made it so I at least had *one* useful thing in there.

Not totally fair, because I truly couldn't live without my lip balm—yes, I was a police officer; no, I hadn't completely forgotten how to be a woman—and that was inside my black leather bag. But, aside from my ID and my cell phone, there wasn't anything else useful.

Except . . . for the snacks I always packed.

A woman never knew when she might get hangry.

I almost laughed out loud.

This was so like me. Make an all-out declaration—even a mental one—and then find all the ways to undermine it.

I can't take off work to go to Maggie's engagement party in California.

But they have Disneyland. And beaches. And Death Valley. And—

Okay, I'll take a vacation out of the bank of days I never actually use, dip into my savings because I can get mouse ears and see some cacti.

So really, the last thing I needed was to go back and encounter Talbot.

It would start off with something like, *He's one of the biggest movie stars on the planet, I can't possibly think that he might be interested in me.* To *he seems really nice and is a good friend to Maggie.* To *let me pledge to this man my undying love, no matter that he'll probably shred my heart into tiny little pieces in the process.*

See?

Dangerous man.

Or perhaps, *I* was the dangerous one. As in being dangerous to myself, being so damned tempted to undermine the safeguards I'd put into place.

Yup. That, too.

Rolling my shoulders, I approached the gate and waved at the security guard. "Can I get out? My car's down the road."

He nodded, cracked the gate enough so I could slip out.

"Hey." Fingers caught my arm, and I resisted the urge to immediately knock them off, instead turning to see Talbot.

My body knew his, even before I recognized his voice, heat curling in my abdomen, flaring out to my fingertips, making my breath catch in my lungs, my lips tingle. "Hi," I said, keeping my tone formal through pure dint of strength. "Did you need something?"

A smile that threatened to melt my bones from the inside out. "Yeah."

I lifted my brows, waited.

"Well, you going to tell me what that is?" I asked with impatience when he just kept looking at me.

"Yeah," he said again.

And still just staring at me.

I spun to leave, this time my movement knocking his hand free.

"A ride," he said, just as I stepped through the gate.

My feet froze, and I slowly turned back. "A ride?" I repeated. He nodded. "To where?" I asked suspiciously.

"My home."

Alarm bells, all *sorts* of alarm bells began to blare in my mind.

"Didn't you drive here?"

A shrug. "I think I drank too much. An officer such as yourself wouldn't want an inebriated driver on the road, would you?"

I knew he was playing me.

But I couldn't think of anything to say that might get me out of spending however long it might take to drive this man home, so in the end, I just nodded and started walking again, my heels *click-clicking* on the pavement.

And Talbot walked silently next to me, not saying another word. Yet I couldn't help but continue to peek out of the corner of my eye and watch him as he glanced up at the sky, the clouds making most of it hazy, the stars dreamily blinking behind the gray swathe. The moon was beautiful, though, shining golden and bright through the drape of atmosphere, and I could understand why he kept looking up.

"It reminds me of home," I whispered.

"The sky?" he asked.

I nodded. "It's so big sometimes, the moon so bright, that it's easy to get lost in the glimmers, to try to track every one of them with my eyes." A chuckle. "Even though I think it would take me a lifetime to attempt it."

He was quiet for several moments, then, "On nights like this, when the smog clears and there's nothing but the night sky, even cloudy, I remember being a little kid and feeling the same way."

A little kid.

He hadn't meant it as an insult, I knew that much. He wasn't a jerk, wouldn't intentionally make me feel bad.

But it did all the same.

Because it was another reminder that I was a backward non-Hollywood type, thinking and feeling the way this man had when he was a *child*. And I hated that I felt that way, that I felt insecure. I knew who I was, and I was fine with that.

I cleared my throat. "How far away do you live?"

Silence.

Then fingers on my arm, not holding me in place, but brushing lightly over the back of my arm. "What did I say?" he asked.

I blinked. "I don't know what you're talking about."

Those fingers wrapped around my wrist, exerted the barest amount of pressure. "I hurt your feelings."

Laughter, forced, escaped my lips. "No, you didn't. I'm just tired and ready to be in my hotel room."

"Hmm."

But he didn't say anything further as we approached my rental and I bleeped the locks. I started to reach for the handle, only his hand was there before mine, and my fingers brushed the hot skin there as he tugged the door open.

I have to admit that I froze.

I wasn't used to men opening doors for me. I did that myself, and it wasn't like my colleagues were dashing in front of me to let me into my squad car.

"Did you . . . want to get in?" he asked softly, making me realize that I'd been standing there making a fool out of myself. Again.

Ugh.

I straightened my shoulders, sank down in the driver's seat, and I made a promise right there and then that there would be no more insecurities. I'd had my couple of hours of discomfort and self-doubt, and that was more than enough. Time to pull my shit together.

And I was doing that . . . right around the moment Talbot leaned over me and buckled my seat belt.

All the air froze in my lungs, a large inhale that captured his spicy scent inside me. Soft fingers on my cheek drove my exhale forth, losing that breath, bringing my lips very close to his.

"You have the prettiest eyes I've ever seen," he murmured.

More breath sliding out of me. My heart thundering in my chest, my lips parting, and . . . then he was gone.

Or not so much gone as out of the car, crossing around in front of it before lowering himself into the passenger's seat.

I cleared my throat, turned on the ignition, then handed him my phone.

"Plug in your address?"

He took it. "What's the code to unlock it?"

I tilted the screen so it captured my face and made it so he could access the apps.

"Privacy is important to you, then?" he asked, his fingers tapping.

"Considering I don't know you?" I returned with a raised brow. "Yes, privacy is important to me, especially with men who try to see unsuspecting women in their underwear."

A chuckle. "I thought we'd covered this already. You were the one bringing the unwanted stripping."

Unwanted.

Ouch.

"But certainly not unappreciated," he said, lifting the phone and setting it in the cradle that was clipped to the air vent. "Just not my preferred way to meet a beautiful woman."

I snorted. Oh, that was rich.

"Yeah?" I said, memorizing the first couple of steps of the navigation before checking for traffic and pulling out onto the road. "What's your preferred way?"

"A quiet dinner at my house, followed by a walk through the garden."

My eyes darted to his, and I bit back another snort. "What, are you a hundred?"

His lips tipped up, one dimple appearing in the cheek I could see. "No," he said. "I'm thirty-six. What about you?"

"I'm . . . not interested in getting to know you any further."

"Ah, I see."

"What do you see?" I asked, navigating the car around a winding turn.

"That it's rude to ask a lady her age." He shifted in his seat, and I could feel him looking at me, even though I couldn't take my eyes off the road to look at him. I did, however, roll them, because . . . seriously? *It's rude to ask a lady her age?* "Also," he murmured before I could go too far down that particular tangent, folding his hands on his lap, "I happen to think that dinner and a walk are a perfectly normal way to get to know someone."

"What about the movies? Or going out to eat? Or—" I stopped, grasping that this man probably couldn't easily do either of those things. "Never mind."

"What?" he asked.

"I just realized that you probably can't really go out much and meet people, huh?"

He was quiet as I drove for a few minutes.

Then he said, "No, I can't head to the movies all that often. Every once in a while, depending on where I'm at, I can sneak into a theater, but definitely not here in L.A. In fact," he added. "It's part of why I'm moving soon. The paparazzi are just all over my house."

A pang of sympathy slid through me.

"That has to be hard," I said, "not being able to go where you want, when you want."

He shrugged, much more cavalier than I would have been if my life had been limited in such a manner. "That's the price you pay to be in movies," he said. "I'm lucky that I've found the success that I have, considering the way the industry has changed in the last few years with streaming. A lot of that is due to Mags, though." I caught another flash of his dimple. "She took me on when she didn't have to, and I'll be grateful to her forever."

"Mags is a great person," I agreed. "I'm glad she's found a job that makes her happy."

"And a man," he pointed out.

I sniffed.

"You don't agree?"

"Oh no," I said. "Aaron is a good guy, and I'm thrilled they found their way back to each other."

"Then what?"

"I learned a long time ago that you can never look at another person as your source for happiness," I said, turning onto the on-ramp and navigating my way onto the freeway.

Quiet from his side of the car.

But then he nodded. "That's the smartest thing I've heard in a long time."

"Well, I'm so glad you think so."

"Do you survive only on sarcasm and barbed retorts?"

"You forgot to include coffee and chocolate glazed donuts."

He stared at me, and this time I couldn't stop myself from glancing away from the road to meet his golden eyes. "Isn't that a little cliché for a cop?"

Laughter bubbled out of me. "Probably." A shrug. "But I like them anyway."

That dimple flashed again. "I'll remember that."

"Why?" I asked suspiciously.

"Because I'll need to pay you back for the ride."

"Yeah, that's not happening."

He shifted in his seat, turning so the front of his body faced me. Not that I was looking. Nope. No way. I didn't need to look to remember the man's delicious chest, and I certainly didn't need to look in order to see his sexy smile. "Why not?" he asked.

It took me a moment to deviate from my thoughts of smiles and yummy chests in order to process his question. "I didn't give you a ride because I expected something in return."

Silence.

For a long time.

"Why did you do it then?"

Good question.

Because part of me had wanted to spend more time with this man, part of me had craved to be in his presence, and because . . . well, a small part (and also the only part I could say out loud because the other two were just . . . okay, they were definitely pathetic considering who I was and who he was) of the reason I had helped him was because I was a decent person, he needed a ride, and he was Maggie's friend.

Which I told him.

Which then resulted in more silence.

Silence that was so long and clawing so deeply at my insides that I found myself having to turn on the radio in order to relieve it.

I found a nice poppy station, full of sugar and cotton candy and catchy choruses, and listened as we drove toward his house. In mileage, it wasn't far from Artie and Pierce's, but in what I was learning about L.A., that didn't necessarily mean that it wouldn't take a long time.

Through stop-and-go traffic.

At eight o'clock at night.

"This is a little different from home," he said, finally popping the seal on the conversation again and turning down the song.

I smacked his hand away. "It is a crime to turn down Lizzo."

His brows rose. "Seriously?"

I didn't even dignify that question with a reply. Instead, I just ignored him as the chorus went on, as the hair-tossing lyrics went on, as the anthem hit its peak, and then when it had slowed and blended into the next song, I turned off the radio, glanced at him expectantly.

"I was just saying that this traffic must be different from home."

I nodded. "Not from the big cities I've lived in, but from Darlington, definitely. I think the big hoopla at the last city council meeting was that we were adding a tenth stoplight in town."

He chuckled. "That's a little different from L.A."

"I can imagine."

"Where else have you lived?"

"Pardon?" I asked, finally seeing the exit that would take us off this godforsaken freeway, and pushing, shoving, and cramming my car into the next lane—much to the anger of the cars behind me, their horns a cheerful melody—so we could exit.

"You don't drive like you're from a small town."

I smiled. "Well, I've done stints in Denver, Salt Lake City, and a year in Chicago."

"Why does the last sound like you're chewing glass."

"Because it's a beautiful city, but it's damned cold." I shuddered. "I barely survived my first—and only—winter there."

"Says the girl who grew up in snowy Utah."

"Says the girl who is definitely not feeling the windchill."

He laughed, and I found myself doing the same. Despite the chip on my shoulder, despite the alarm bells blaring in my mind, telling me to gather up armor and slap it on every part of me, to protect every vulnerable inch.

I laughed.

And for a moment, I forgot he was a big, fancy movie star and I was just a small-town woman, who dreamed of Disney and glazed donuts and a vat of coffee, black.

"Did you just grow up here then?"

He nodded. "In California, yes, but in the northern part, a

suburb south of San Francisco." A shrug. "Not a small town, exactly, but certainly not a big city like down here."

"How'd you get into acting?" I found myself asking.

"How'd you get into being a police officer?" he countered.

"Tit for tat?"

A smile that hit me right in the gut. "Seems only fair."

"My dad was a police officer, seemed fitting to follow in his footsteps."

"What about your mom's footsteps?"

That question stung. He couldn't have known that, of course, but it still burned like acid dripping down my skin. I cleared my throat. "Nice try," I said, forcing my tone to be light. "But you didn't answer my question."

"I got into acting because I needed to escape my childhood."

I blinked, his reply pretty much the last thing I'd expected to hear, and certainly not with such a neutral tone. "That's a bomb to drop in the middle of the getting-to-know-you conversation," I murmured.

"You mean, you didn't know?"

"Know what?" I asked, my brows pulling down.

"Know about my childhood."

The light turned red, and I took the opportunity to study him closely. "Why would I know about your childhood?"

His gold eyes flared.

But he didn't answer me, and then the light turned green, and I needed to pull forward.

"Because it seems like all of America knows about it."

The soft sentence took me by surprise, and I thought carefully, trying to recall if I did know something. But . . . I liked a good action flick now and then, had certainly seen this man in a film or two, but I didn't know anything about his personal life.

"I'm not one for gossip rags," I said. "Darlington has its own gossip patrol, and I have enough to keep track of with Lilibeth's mail thief, whoever toilet papered the elementary school playground, and the Milk Caper."

I don't know what he'd been planning on saying before I'd finished.

But it certainly wasn't the same thing as what came out of his mouth next.

"The Milk Caper?" he asked.

"Don't ask," I told him. "It's a long, drawn-out story, and one that's barely interesting."

"With a name like the Milk Caper, I doubt that."

Regardless of his doubts, we were turning into his driveway, and I was saved from having to explain about little Tommy Brighton—all of six years old—and his mysterious milk guzzling abilities. The supermarket hadn't been able to figure out where the milk was going—Tommy had been taught to clean up after himself, like a good kiddo—and so the gallons (yes, *gallons*) of milk had disappeared for weeks on end.

Until his dad, Mark, the owner of the grocery store, had set up a hidden camera and had caught his son in the act in between school and his afternoon nap.

Ah, to be a police officer in Darlington.

Though, I had to admit, I liked tracking down a Milk Caper much more than the drug busts from a few years back.

So long as I wasn't the one who had to clean up the toilet paper from the playground.

I pulled up to the gate, turned to him.

"It's 7-7-1-9-2," he said, and I lifted a brow. His lips turned up. "Consider this my play at getting a beautiful woman to have dinner with me and to maybe go on a walk afterward."

"You're unbelievable."

"I'm taking that as a compliment."

"You shouldn't."

He laughed and squeezed my hand where it rested on the steering wheel. "I can get out here," he said, popping the door and unbuckling his seat belt.

I quickly put the car in park.

Then, for some reason, I got out.

Later, I wouldn't be able to pinpoint why exactly, except to say that perhaps it was some kind of instinct bred from years of training, but either way, I *did* get out, shifting back so he could squeeze between the car and the code box.

He started to plug in numbers, and I saw 7-7-1-9—

But then I saw something else.

Movement out of the corner of my eye. Someone coming up fast, and—a flicker of silver, metal gleaming in the moonlight—I reached under my dress, yanked out my gun, and ordered, "Behind me."

"What?" Talbot asked.

I yanked him back from the box, put his body between mine and the car, then leveled my gun in the direction of the threat.

There was an ear-piercing scream as a man appeared out of the bushes, a knife raised above his head—

I fired.

Once.

The man got up, and the blade whizzed near enough by my head that I felt the rush of hair flying by my ear.

Then I felt the sting of that blade hitting my skin.

And I fired again. Then again. And . . . finally, the man collapsed.

I kicked the knife away, knelt next to him, my hands going to the wounds and putting as much pressure as I could muster before my gaze shot back to Talbot's. He was uninjured, his face pale, his expression one of utter shock.

"Call 9-1-1," I ordered, just as a flash of light nearly blinded me.

He reached for his cell, more flashes coming.

I looked in the other direction, and I saw a good dozen cameras pointed my way.

At me *and* Talbot.

One instant.

One reaction.

And I knew my life had just changed forever.

CHAPTER FIVE

Talbot

I WAS AN ACTOR.

I'd played a cop a few times.

But I was just an actor.

So, seeing what Tammy had just done left me shaken as I ran to the house for some towels to staunch the bleeding.

She'd moved . . . like liquid lightning.

Beautiful, capable, liquid lightning. One second, I'd been punching in my code, and the next . . . she'd been fighting off a knife-wielding man with her gun. A man whose life she was now trying to save.

I barreled up to my front door, my fingers shaking when I pressed the code into the keypad, my breaths coming in short, staccato bursts.

Then I was inside, lurching toward the half-bath just off the hall, grabbing all the towels I could find, and hauling ass back toward the front gate. Tammy was there, still on her knees, still with her hands over the man's chest.

They were covered in blood, and I swallowed down a sudden burst of nausea before kneeling next to her.

"What do you need?"

"Put some here"—she nodded toward the man's chest—"then fold one up and put it under his head."

The flashes were still coming, all except from a slender brunette, her camera slung over her shoulder. She was the same paparazzo who'd told me that she'd already called 9-1-1, walking through the flashes to come stand next to Tammy.

"Here," she said now, taking a towel and carefully placing it under the man's head. Then grabbing another and using it to pick up the knife Tammy had knocked away from the attacker. "So it doesn't walk away," she murmured before stepping back again.

But I noticed that she didn't pick up her camera, wasn't shooting the gory scene like her compatriots.

Before I had a chance to consider that too closely, Tammy cursed, and I glanced down to see that the towels had soaked through. Quickly, I set another one on the man's chest, used my hands next to hers to add more pressure.

Thankfully, I heard sirens in the distance, the blaring coming nearer.

An ambulance screeched into the drive less than a minute later, the medics appearing quickly, bags in hand.

"Male, mid-thirties, three gunshot wounds, two to the torso, one to the right arm," Tammy said. "He's lost a lot of blood, and his pulse is there, but thready."

They took over, attempting to staunch the bleeding, administering drugs, then quickly loading him on a stretcher. But even as I watched that, the police rolled up, sirens loud enough to make me wince, flashing lights even brighter than the paparazzi's.

Tammy had retrieved her badge, holding it up so they could examine it, and then quickly turning over her gun as she explained what happened.

They nodded, glanced from the gun to Tammy to me to the

paparazzi, and then one of the officers stepped forward. "Let's take this into the house."

———

HER HANDS WERE COVERED with blood.

I glanced down, saw that my hands were equally coated as well, and felt bile burn the back of my throat.

Tammy was talking to the officer, who had urged us into the house, and he was taking notes on a pad as she stood there in her dress and heels with scraped knees.

And blood-covered hands.

I barely bit back my gag reflex.

Tammy's head spun, her eyes locking with mine for one brief, intense moment, and then she was saying something to the policeman, before he nodded, and she crossed over to me.

"Are you okay?" I asked.

"Fine," she clipped, snagging my arm and bringing me over to the large kitchen sink. The water turned on . . . and then she was scrubbing my hands in the sink, the stream turning pink then red then back to pink, until eventually it ran clear again. Soap into her palms, rubbing over mine, rubbing firmly until both of our hands were clean.

"There," she whispered, snagging a towel and running it over my fingers and wrists. "Why don't you sit down?"

My eyes were on my hands, on hers. "I'm okay," I said.

Fingers on my jaw, drawing my gaze up to hers, those hazel depths searching mine, seeming to scour my very soul. Then she nodded and started to turn away.

And that's when I saw the blood on her arm.

The *gash* on her arm.

My heart skipped, thudding in my chest, slamming against my ribs. She'd gotten hurt protecting me.

The bile disappeared. The shock flitted away.

Rage took its place.

"Your arm," I said, snagging her wrist, drawing her to a stop.

"It's fine," she said, glancing back at me over her shoulder. "The medics gave me some gauze earlier to stop the bleeding. I'll get it looked at when I'm done giving my statement." A beat. "You'll need to give yours next. Unless you need to call in a lawyer?"

Gauze? *Gauze?*

She slipped her wrist free, raised her brows. "Do you need to call someone?"

I shook my head. "I don't need a lawyer for this."

At least, I didn't think so. It wasn't like either of us had done anything wrong, and certainly the mob of paparazzi could corroborate what had happened. I might need Maggie and her magical PR skills, but I wasn't going to ruin the night of her engagement party with a scandal.

Although . . . I pulled my cell from my pocket, fired off a text asking her to call me.

Because if I'd learned anything about my friend in the years we'd worked together, it was that she hated to be blindsided— and she would hate even more to wake up tomorrow and be taken by surprise with the events of this evening plastered all over every gossip mag and site, not to mention the main-stream news outlets.

The text would cover my bases.

And hopefully, she would see it after the party but before morning.

Tammy was talking to the officer by the time I finished texting, so I slipped down the hall and into the half-bath I'd stripped of all things towel just a little while before. There was a first aid kit beneath the sink, and I grabbed it, bringing it back into the kitchen and opening it up. More gauze. A wrap.

At least I could get it covered until Tammy had it checked out.

The last of which had me remembering a contact I'd

programmed in my cell just the previous week. On Artie and Pierce's recommendation, I'd signed up for a doctor's service—it was easier than going into medical offices or the hospital (for non-emergency stuff)—and there was a direct number for urgent visits.

I stepped into the hall and called.

The calm, kind voice on the other end said they would be here in twenty minutes.

Feeling better about having done *something*, I told them to call my number when they arrived, so I could let them in, then went back into the kitchen and put on a pot of coffee. By the sound of the conversation Tammy was having with the officer, it seemed like they might be at it for a while, and then there was her arm to consider, how long it would take to treat it. We would probably be up for hours.

Plus, it gave me something to do that wasn't standing around, staring into space, hating myself for freezing, and furious that she had gotten hurt protecting me.

The coffee steam hissed its way out of the pot, and I grabbed three mugs, filling them and bringing two of them to the officer and Tammy. The first took the mug gratefully. The second with no little amount of suspicion.

"Did you need cream or sugar?"

She shook her head, took a small sip, and I could have sworn that her eyes gentled. Then she was nodding at the cop and saying, "Talbot, this is Officer McTavish. He's going to take your statement, if you're ready."

"Of course," I said.

"Bill," he said, extending his hand. "Feel free to just call me Bill."

I nodded.

He gestured to the barstools. "Did you want to sit down?"

"No," I told him, "I'm okay. What did you need to know?"

"Let's start at the beginning. Do you know about what time you pulled up to the gate?"

"Um, maybe a few minutes after ten?" I tried to think back, but I hadn't really been paying attention to the time. I'd been too enthralled with the woman sitting in the car next to me. "I left the party early and saw Tammy, and since my car was blocked in and I'd had a couple of drinks, I asked her for a ride. My place is . . . thirty minutes or so from Artie and Pierce's without traffic, but we did hit the usual slowdown on the freeway for a few miles."

He nodded.

And then asked another question. And another.

And by the time I'd related even the most innocuous detail about the drive and that stop-and-go traffic and the winding road up to my house, finally reaching the part of the story where I'd been putting in my gate code, my cell rang.

I glanced down at the screen. "Sorry," I said. "I think that must be the doctor."

"Go ahead."

I picked up, got confirmation it was, in fact, the doctor, and said, "I'll come down and let you in."

Bill snagged my forearm. "I can radio down. They'll escort him up."

I nodded, relayed that information, and hung up. Then I told Bill, "It's actually her. Dr. Bailey Stevens. She says she has her ID."

After calling that into his radio, he said, "So, you'd put the code in . . ."

"Part of it, yes. But I hadn't finished when Tammy whipped around, pushing me between her and the car. At first, I didn't see anything, but then I caught a flash of silver and saw the man coming toward us. I heard her tell him to stop, but he didn't. Then she fired." My heart began pounding again in my chest, and I took a breath, forced it to slow. "He got back up, and she fired again. Two times."

"Then what happened?"

"He didn't get back up, so she kicked the knife away, ordered me to call 9-1-1 and to get some towels—"

The knock at the door interrupted me.

"I'll be right back," I said.

Bill nodded.

I went to answer the door, or rather to follow Tammy down the hall as she pulled it open.

A petite brunette wearing a plaid button-down and blue jeans stood on the porch. She held a large bag with one hand, an ID in the other.

"Who are you?" Tammy asked, and I'd be lying if the protectiveness in her tone didn't make my heart skip a beat.

"I'm Dr. Stev—"

I moved, some instinct bringing me to Tammy's side in an instant.

It was a good thing, too.

Because she went gray, her legs buckled, and I snagged her arm before her head could crack into the frame, tugging her body against mine.

She tried to shrug me off. "I'm fine."

"You don't look fine."

"I *am* fi—"

A sentiment that was cut off by her passing out, going completely limp in my hold. I moved quickly, slipping one arm beneath her knees, shifting the other to her shoulders, and hoisting her up against my chest.

"She's the injured one," I told the doctor needlessly.

To her credit, Dr. Stevens didn't blink, just said, "Let's get her inside."

I turned around but not before I saw another camera flash.

And I knew—*just knew*—that Maggie was going to kill me for not calling her.

CHAPTER SIX

Tammy

I WOKE to a strange tugging at my arm, muffled voices in the background.

For a moment, I thought I was back home, back in Darlington, my adorable twin nieces having snuck into my house and attempting to wake me.

But, for one, the mattress I was lying on was much more comfortable than my own, and for another, the voices in the background were male.

"Easy," came a female voice, and my eyes flashed open to see a woman holding a needle and a pair of scissors in either hand. "I'm Dr. Stevens," she said. "You have quite a nasty gash, but I'm nearly done stitching it up. How are you feeling?"

Exhausted for one.

Weak for another.

But that was just the adrenaline coming down, or perhaps it was from the loss of blood. The cut had soaked through most of the gauze the paramedic had given me before I'd finally managed to get it to stop.

"I'm fine."

A smile. "You good with me finishing up?"

I nodded, directed my eyes away from my arm, and tried to ignore the tugging when it resumed.

"You were asleep for the cleaning part," she said lightly. "Lucky for you. But I do want to put you on some hefty antibiotics, just in case that blade was dirtier than it looked. As for blood loss, you lost quite a bit, but as long as you take it easy for the next couple of days, you should bounce back quickly."

Well, there went my trip to the happiest place on Earth.

I made a face.

She laughed, patted my hand. "It's not so bad, I promise."

"I'm here on vacation," I said, turning back in time to see her snip the thread—or whatever material it was that doctors used to stitch people up—and set the instruments aside.

"Knife wound as a souvenir. That sucks."

I snorted.

She patted my hand again. "Though, what doesn't suck is having that man go all protective and growly over you." Her head inclined toward Talbot, and I followed her gaze, saw he was watching me while speaking to Officer McTavish again.

"What do you mean?" I asked, glancing back.

Her brows lifted. "You'd have thought the man had the queen in his arms when you passed out." She tugged off her gloves. "And I don't mean to make light of it, because clearly, you're a person who deserves care, but I don't think Talbot Green is going to forget what you did for him any time soon."

Shock made it so no words came.

Not that it mattered as Dr. Stevens began relaying information for me, writing me out a prescription for antibiotics (after shooing the men out so she could give me a shot of them in my ass, joy of joys). Then she took down my email so she could email me instructions, waved off my offer of my health insurance *and* my credit card, saying it was already taken care of.

Then she packed up her bag, patted my hand for a third time, and left.

The men weren't back yet, and I was alone, lying in a bed that wasn't my own, in a giant room with flowy furnishings along with a humungous TV on one wall, and trying to reconcile the image of Talbot being protective and growly.

Over *me*. A woman he hardly knew.

It just didn't fit in with the flirtatious, teasing man from the garden and car ride, nor with the stunned one in the aftermath of the attack.

He'd been so quiet, so withdrawn.

So . . . protective? Growly?

Um, what?

That just didn't compute.

A soft knock had me looking up, tearing my gaze from the large painting of birch trees adorning one long wall over to the door.

"Hey," Talbot said when I met his eyes. "How are you feeling?"

Besides the throbbing in my arm and the swishing sensation in my brain? I was just peachy. I also needed to find a way to get out of here and back to my hotel. I'd stay in bed, order room service, and veg out on bad television.

Kind of what I'd do if I were home alone.

Only paying two hundred and fifty bucks a night to do it.

Not the point.

"I'm great," I said, pushing my elbows beneath me. "I should probably go."

He shook his head.

I frowned.

"You can't go anywhere for the next few hours, at least. They're still processing the crime scene, and that's not even considering the paparazzi camped out there. You'd be overrun in just a few seconds." A sharp shake of his head. "I need to get you security."

I plunked my feet onto the floor. "I can take care of myself."

Golden eyes on mine. "That, I know." He crossed over to

me, dropped a hand on my shoulder before I could stand, keeping my ass on the comfy mattress. "And me, too, apparently." His expression was filled with remorse. "I'm so sorry you were here and got caught up in this."

"I'm not."

He blinked.

"If I weren't here, something bad might have happened." He made a noise of protest, and I amended my statement. "Something worse might have happened."

"You were hurt protecting me."

And there was a hint of a growl.

Interesting.

Also interesting was the way it sent a ribbon of desire through me, curling in my abdomen, dragging over my skin like heated silk.

I lifted my chin. "It's my job to protect people."

"You could have been killed."

"So could you."

Talbot stopped, considered that, then abruptly shook his head, nudging me to lie back on the mattress again. Normally, I would have never allowed it, but my head was still a bit fuzzy and my arm was starting to hurt in earnest.

"I'm going to grab you pain medicine and some food to put in your stomach. You're going to keep that adorable, sexy, competent ass in my bed. Otherwise, I'll rustle up some handcuffs and see how you like being on the receiving end of them."

Then he was gone, sweeping from the room in a flurry of male fury.

"My bed?" I mouthed, my eyes taking in the space under a whole new lens. His bed. *Talbot's* bed.

Talbot's. Bed.

Sweet Christ.

In fact, that detail took me so long to process—I was blaming the aching arm and swirling head and not that curl of heat in my stomach, between my thighs—that I hardly processed the order, the threat of handcuffs.

Until I did.

"Motherfucker," I hissed, shoving myself up again and seeing that my feet were bare, taking a moment to let my brain settle before I searched the room for my shoes.

There.

Lined up neatly by the door.

Squinting against my eddying vision, I took a few deep breaths. "Thinks he can give me orders," I muttered. "As *fucking* if."

But my eyes didn't clear, and my arm was hurting more by the minute.

Clearly, even if my car wasn't part of a crime scene, I couldn't safely drive.

"What did I say?"

It was a snapped-out question, one that was paired with Talbot stalking across the room, setting a mug of what smelled like tea on the nightstand, along with toast covered in cinnamon and sugar.

Both of which smelled delicious.

Not that it mattered.

I needed to get out of here. Because the longer I spent in this man's presence, the more I was at risk of remembering who he was . . . and who I was. I needed to call a Lyft. STAT.

"Don't touch me," I said, doing some snapping of my own when he went to no doubt nudge me back onto the mattress again.

He lifted his hands, though those golden eyes were heated to molten metal. "You look like you're going to pass out," he growled. Yes. Growled, and I was momentarily stunned by how lovely that rasping sound felt as it flitted through the airwaves, brushed lightly over my skin.

"I'm fine," I said. "I just need to get back to my hotel and sleep it off."

He laughed, loud and long, and it was a fucking beautiful sound.

"What?" I asked when he'd quieted.

"You are absolutely fucking insane if you think that I'm letting you leave when you're like this. You can't drive—"

"I didn't say I was going to," I muttered.

"Hell, if I called a car for you, you'd pass out in the back seat before you even had the chance to make it to your hotel." His voice gentled, those eyes turning more into sunshine than metal. "You need to eat a little something so you can take the pain meds, and then you need to rest."

"I'm not taking drugs from a stranger."

A brow lifting, a perfect arched rainbow above the shining sun of his eyes. "I could hardly be considered a stranger," he muttered. "I've known Maggie for years."

That was true.

But *I* didn't know this man.

"Should I call Dr. Stevens back? Will you trust the medication if it's from a doctor?" He pulled out his cell. "Or Maggie?"

"No," I said quickly. "Don't ruin Maggie's night. She was having such a good time, and I don't want her to worry or to leave. She deserves this." And I didn't want to ruin it, especially when she and Aaron's road to their happy ending had been so long and arduous.

"Okay," he said. "So, I'll get Dr. Stevens to come back."

Shit.

And make the poor woman turn around this late at night?

"No," I said. "Don't do that, either."

He knelt by the bed. "Then what do you want to do?"

My heart prickled. My eyes narrowed.

"Because obviously," he pointed out, "if you won't let me call Mags or Dr. Stevens, we're at a stalemate."

I resisted the urge to cross my arms.

"I'm not going to force the pain pills down your throat."

As if he even could.

And yes, that was delusion talking, considering this man could easily overpower me in my current state.

"I can FaceTime Dr. Stevens to confirm the pills are from her."

I wrinkled my nose.

"I can promise they are, in fact, just pain pills and not some sort of illicit drug."

"And that is exactly what an illicit drug dealer would say," I muttered.

"So, FaceTime with the good doctor then?"

"No," I muttered, grabbing the pill bottle from the nightstand and squinting to read the label with my still-hazy vision. Oxycontin, ten milligrams every four hours, and the issuer was Dr. Stevens. "What?" I asked, still muttering. "Does she give this stuff out like candy?"

"Don't know," he said. "This was the first time I've used her, but considering that there are only enough pills in there for three days, I doubt it."

I kept squinting, saw that indeed the number eighteen was written under quantity. Then sighed and knew I'd lost this battle. My arm felt like it had gone six rounds with a flamethrower, and fatigue was creeping in to join my stuffing-filled head. I needed food, pills, and sleep.

In that order, even if my body was telling me that I needed it in the opposite.

"What'd you poison the toast with?" I grumbled, setting the pill bottle down and picking up one of the pieces.

"Only a little arsenic," he said, playing along.

I chuckled, even though I didn't want to. "Tasty," I said dryly.

"I did my best. My personal chef has the night off."

The toast stopped two inches from my mouth, my eyebrow went up.

"I'm kidding," he said. "I like to cook." A shrug. "I do have someone stock my fridge for me so it's full when I'm home. But no chef."

Hmm.

His fingers circled my wrist, pushed it closer to my mouth. "Eat, sweetheart."

Flutters in my stomach, need sliding up my arm making my breasts go all tingly, my nipples harden against my bra, and I opened my lips, wanting to say something, to tell him not to call me sweetheart. But his hand was still moving mine, and the next thing I knew, the toast was in my mouth and I was taking a bite.

"Mmm," I moaned.

God, it had been so long since I'd had this simple snack, and I'd forgotten how incredible it was.

"Good?" he asked.

I nodded, plowed my way through that slice, still sitting on the edge of the bed, Talbot still on his knees in front of me.

He picked up the mug of tea, passed it over. "Also, not poisoned," he said before I could even come up with a protest to not accept it. Not that I could, the floral and spice scent was like nirvana, tempting my fingers to wrap around the warm ceramic. "Got it?" he asked, before taking his hand away.

"Yes," I breathed, lifting it to my lips and drinking deeply.

After I'd sipped for a bit, he took it back, swapped it with the plate for the second piece of toast. Which I devoured, too.

"My mom used to make this for me," I whispered.

Then immediately wished I could take back the words. I hadn't thought about my mom in a long time. Not since—

"Mine, too," he said softly. "When she was sober, that is." Said so offhandedly that I immediately understood this was part of the whole shitty childhood that the whole world seemed to know—all except for me. Talbot's shoulders lifted and fell in a small shrug. "I don't know why, but it always tastes better when someone else makes it for you."

That was true.

"Do your parents still live in Darlington?" he asked, before I could formulate anything other than a nod.

I shook my head. "They died quite a few years ago now."

"I'm sorry." His hand rested lightly on my knee, careful to not touch the abrasions, I realized, but not so high as to make me uncomfortable. The man had skills, that was for damned sure.

"Like I said"—I reached for the bottle of pills—"it's been years now."

"Doesn't mean that stuff just goes away."

"Trust me," I said. "Sometimes it's better that we pretend it just does."

He went still. Very, very still. Then he reached for the mug, handing it to me when I took a pill out of the bottle and stuck it in my mouth.

I drank, swallowed it down. "Just saying, I'll kill you if these are illicit drugs."

"Noted," he said, lips twitching as he set it on the nightstand again and stood up, moving to another door and disappearing through it, only to emerge a few moments later with a T-shirt and sweats in his hands. Then he knelt in front of me again, his hands on my knees once more, only this time his words made my lungs seize, my pulse flutter.

"Do you need help changing?"

CHAPTER SEVEN

Talbot

IF SHE'D HAD her gun, I might have been her next target.

But luckily for me, she didn't.

So I just stayed where I was, hands just above the cuts on her knees and staring into her pretty hazel eyes.

I'd gone straight past any hesitation about her being Maggie's friend and dove headfirst into the deep end. This woman had saved my life. This woman had bled for me. This woman with the shadows in her eyes and the chip on her shoulder . . . she was mine.

And I was going to take care of her.

Even if she fought me every step of the way.

Like right now, the protest bubbling up in her throat.

"I won't look," I promised, even though I sort of hated myself for it. "But you need to get out of that dress. It's dirty."

Sparking, furious hazel eyes.

It was funny. I hardly knew this woman, and yet I *did* know her. I knew that the look she was giving me meant she had a rebuke, an argument, on the tip of her tongue, and she was ready to unleash it on me. I also knew this woman wasn't unreasonable. She'd deferred to logic more than once already.

So, I knew she'd eventually come around.

"I'm sure you want something comfortable to sleep in," I added, keeping my tone even and gentle. "And," I added, "I *did* mean it when I said I wouldn't look."

A snort. "Like you didn't look earlier?"

"I didn't promise *not* to look earlier." I held her stare. "This time, I am."

Three, two, one. A sigh.

And I knew I had her.

"Fine," she muttered. "But I swear to God, if I catch one flicker of those gorgeous golden eyes on me, I'll put my hand-to-hand combat skills to use."

My thumb traced light circles on the skin just beneath the hem of her dress. "You think my eyes are gorgeous?"

Another sigh. "That's all you absorbed from my statement? That you have pretty eyes?" Hers came to mine. "Yes, Tal. I think your eyes are absolutely beautiful, and I'm sure you've been told that plenty of times before."

I had.

But not by *this* woman.

Also, not in that begrudging way, as though she felt duty-bound to compliment me—which didn't feel as good, but also . . . I'd take any flattery this woman decided to toss in my direction.

"I—" She paused, waited until I was looking at her again. "I also meant what I said about my hand-to-hand combat skills. I will put them to good use, if you so much as put an eyelash out of line."

Considering she appeared ready to pass out, I doubted that. But, I also figured that Tammy wasn't a woman who anyone smart discounted, so instead of commenting on her pale skin and shaking hands, I just nodded. "I made a promise, and I don't ever break promises."

Her lips parted, a flurry of emotions trailing across her face, too fast for me to discern each individual one.

Then I picked up the T-shirt and said, "I won't put any body part, eyelash or otherwise, out of line." I lifted a strand of her long blond hair that was tangled over her face and carefully tucked it behind her ear. "You've exhibited your hand-to-hand skills enough already today, don't you agree?"

Those lips parted again, the bottom one lush and tempting. The top crisscrossed with a tiny white scar through the perfect cupid's bow. Her breath hit my skin, the spice of the tea and toast floating through the air, tempting me with the sweetness hanging on its coattails.

But instead of leaning in, instead of tasting that tantalizing mix of sweet and spice, I straightened, shifting so I could reach around her and unzip the back of her dress. It parted, revealing a narrow strip of black lace, one that matched the glimpse of what I'd seen covering her pussy, disappearing between the tempting curves of her ass, and making me want to forget all about my promise to not look. Especially, when her breath caught as I undid the hooks.

Smooth, golden skin. Lithe muscles. A freckle just there, calling for my mouth.

Slamming my eyes shut, I moved back to the floor. "Can you get them down your shoulders?"

"Yes." I felt her shift on the bed, my imagination going wild, my cock hard and pressing against the zipper of my slacks. Which made me feel like the biggest pervert on the planet—her being injured, drugged, and exhausted. But it wasn't like I was going to take advantage of her.

I just . . . wanted to.

See? Fucking pervert.

Keeping my lids firmly shut, I held up the shirt. "Ready for this?"

A sigh. Then, "No."

"No?"

The air in front of my face shifted, but still I didn't open my eyes.

"You're really not looking, are you?"

"No," I said, but I also felt duty-bound to admit, "Though, I had to look a little when I undid your zipper and bra." A beat. "Also, I really *want* to look, so take that how you want."

Silence.

Then . . . laughter. "You really are the most extraordinary man."

"That's the drugs talking," I deadpanned, waving the shirt. "Ready for this, now?"

"No."

I froze, waited for more of an explanation.

Eventually, she sighed again and said, "Turns out, I can't actually lift my arm to bring the strap down. Any way you can *not* look while helping me?"

No, I fucking couldn't.

I mean, I *would*. But also . . . I couldn't. Fucking hell.

Cock throbbing, I carefully opened my eyes, focused deliberately on her face, and I got up on my knees, bringing our bodies close together, my mouth near enough to hers that I could have easily closed the distance between us, have felt her lush, plump lips on mine, tasted that spice chased by sweet.

But I wasn't a fucking asshole.

So instead of kissing her, I held steady, locked my gaze on hers, and I reached for the straps of her dress and bra.

The moment my fingers brushed the silken skin of her shoulders, a groan crept into the back of my throat, threatened to bubble free, to land in the air between us. Swallowing it down, I forced myself to focus on the task at hand—getting Tammy naked.

No. Dumbass.

My task was to not hurt her as I got her naked.

Stop thinking about her naked.

But that was becoming increasingly hard to do as I eased the straps down, as I kept my eyes on hers, as I continued coaxing the material off her shoulders, along her arms, carefully over the bandage.

And then beyond her elbows, slipping her wrists through, her hands, her fingers free.

Topless.

She was topless, and all I had to do was glance down and I would see a pair of what I knew would be absolutely glorious breasts.

I didn't though, just snagged the T-shirt up from the bed without moving my eyes from hers; the hazel depths deepened to a russet lined with emerald, rings of dark gray at their edges, burning into mine. I fumbled for a few moments, trying to make sure the correct part was forward, and then ultimately deciding it didn't matter, and slipping the shirt over her head.

"Thanks," she whispered, lifting her uninjured arm through the hole and attempting to lift her injured one. Then stopping with a wince.

"Here," I murmured, still soaking in the heat of her eyes, and reached for her wrist and elbow, carefully bringing it up, releasing one hand and tugging the material down. The latter was my mistake because when I reached for the hem of the shirt, the back of my hand brushed over her nipple.

We both gasped.

I swallowed hard, my head going a little fuzzy from the contact.

Then I cleared my throat. "Sorry."

"I-it's okay."

It wasn't. Neither of us was okay, but I didn't say anything further, just gently coaxed her arm through the hole, pausing to roll the short sleeve of the shirt up beyond her bandage wrapped high on her arm so it wouldn't chafe before pulling the shirt down to cover her.

Then I girded my loins, wrapped an arm around her waist, and lifted her up to her feet. Either the drugs were hitting or the exhaustion had overwhelmed her, because her body just leaned loosely against mine, her forehead resting against my collarbone, and I used my free hand to coax the dress to the floor, bringing the shirt along with it.

"Can you lift one leg?" I asked, reaching for the sweats.

Tammy didn't say anything, just leaned heavier against me, raising her foot enough for me to slip one leg of the sweats on. Then the other. A moment later they were around her waist.

Threatening to fall *off* her waist.

I helped her sit, reached for the tie.

Her lips parted again, her breath sliding out. "Tal—"

"Shh, sweetheart," I murmured, making quick work of tying it, before lifting her up, yanking the blankets down, and then tucking her into my bed.

On my side.

Her hair fanned out on my pillow.

My cock still throbbing.

"Talbot?" she asked again, her eyes sliding shut.

"I'll leave a glass of water here," I whispered. "Just rest now, and I'll only be in the next room, so holler if you need anything."

Her eyes stayed closed. Her lips settled closed. But then she gave me the tiniest nod.

Heart aching in a way I didn't completely understand, and yet in a way I also totally understood—because this woman had made a place in my heart in mere hours—I quietly gathered up the plate and the mug, her dirty dress and bra, and headed for the door.

"Talbot?" she said once again, just before I slipped out into the hall.

"Yeah, sweetheart?"

"Thanks." The word barely reached my ears.

"You're welcome."

I turned for the kitchen but heard her next statement all the same.

"Still not your sweetheart."

A grin tugging up my lips, I walked down the hall, took care of the dirty dishes, and then I returned to my bedroom, making sure to leave that glass of water and bottle of pills well within reach.

Except when I started to leave again, when I tried to force my feet to take me into the hall, I found that I couldn't leave her.

Instead, I dragged a chair from the corner of the room close to her bedside, kicked off my shoes, and then watched her sleep.

Watched her breathe.

Understanding that I'd nearly lost something very precious that evening.

Understanding that I hadn't even been the one to save it.

She had.

And me, too.

And I didn't even mean from the armed lunatic.

CHAPTER EIGHT

Tammy

I WOKE, having the sense that it was much later than I would have crawled out of bed for my theme park adventures, wincing when I shifted and stretched, my back pretty much the only comfortable part on my body.

My entire arm was on fire. My knees ached. My head pounded as I slit open my eyes.

Even *they* hurt, probably from the brilliant sunlight pouring in through the windows that took up one length of the huge room. I hadn't noticed them before, seeing as it had been dark, but as I blinked against the bright light, I saw that the room faced some sort of garden space, lush greenery and colorful flowers on the other side of that glass. It really was quite beautiful, reminding me of a lush Hawaiian jungle or something.

Or maybe that was the rest of the space—all light wood and gauzy curtains. The bed had four tall posts going up toward the ceiling, connected by four wooden rails. Like the canopy bed I'd had as a kid.

Only much nicer.

Snorting, I went to put my elbows beneath me, to prop

myself up in a preemptive attack to getting my body moving out of this bed, but the action had me gasping and lying back.

Pain meds first.

I turned my head, saw the promised glass of water, the bottle of pills next to it.

Inching my uninjured arm out, I snagged the bottle and was using my teeth on the child lock top when I heard.

"Need some help?"

I mean, obviously, I needed help. I was gnawing on a bottle of Oxycontin. But when I shifted, my glare already on my face in anticipation of unleashing it on Talbot, I found he wasn't at the door to the hall.

Which drew my gaze farther across the room, past the blond-colored wood entertainment system, past the door to what I presumed was his closet, since he'd disappeared through it and reappeared with clothes the night before, past the lush garden view, and finally . . . settling onto . . .

Heaven.

No, Tammy. Not heaven. It was just—

The man was standing there in all his glory, with nothing but a towel wrapped around his waist, leaning against a doorway—insert more presuming here—that led to the bathroom, considering both that skimpy slip of cotton *and* the fact the man's hair was wet.

I wanted to run my hands through it.

I *wanted* to run my hands over that chest with grabbable pecs, with carefully etched abs, my fingers tingling with so much need that they actually curled taut, making me gasp when my injured arm protested.

Making Talbot move.

He was at the bedside in an instant, taking the bottle from my hand, opening the lid, and shaking out a pill into his palm. "Open," he ordered, and I was too dazed by the Greek god in front of me, kneeling at my side again, this time in only a towel, and in too much pain to argue.

I parted my lips, sipped at the glass when he held it up to my mouth.

"Okay?" he asked a moment later, putting the glass back down when I nodded.

"Thanks," I said.

His fingers brushed lightly over my cheek. "I should be the one thanking you."

"You're still on about that, are you?" I grumbled, the pain in my arm dimming significantly with every touch of his skin against mine. Or maybe it was just some placebo effect.

Take pill. Feel better.

Even though it would take upwards of twenty minutes to be absorbed into my bloodstream.

Except, I had the creeping feeling that the whole feeling better thing came less from the placebo effect or from the touch of his skin (though both were pretty great) and more from the smile on Talbot's face.

I didn't think I'd ever seen one like that before.

Or at least not one like that pointed in my direction.

I'd seen Aaron give it to Maggie. I'd witnessed Pierce give it to Artie.

And now this man . . . to *me*.

What alternate universe had I stumbled into?

Not one that made any sense, that was for damned sure. Or maybe that was the drugs talking, maybe I had a superhuman ability to metabolize them, pain relief instantly hitting my veins, totally unimpacted by Talbot Green.

Yes, I knew I was lying.

But I also was *lying* in a Hollywood superstar's bed, after having been wounded saving his life the night before, with that superstar currently kneeling next to me and *stroking my cheek.*

The entire scenario was like a bad script.

Probably, something that Talbot had seen plenty of.

Those fingers drifted down to my throat, brushing back and forth across the dip in the middle, probably feeling my pulse galloping in my veins, the rapid *thrum-thrum* tapping against his fingertips.

But if he did feel it, he didn't say anything about it.

Instead, his fingers kept moving, and he asked, "Why the smile?"

I scowled.

He chuckled. "You're beautiful when you glare at me, did you know that?"

"*That's* the savior complex coming into play."

His brows drew together. "What are you talking about?"

I went to shrug, just barely stopped myself in time. "It's a normal reaction," I said, making my tone knowing, hoping it would piss him off and get him to back off, because with that soft smile, those gorgeous eyes, the sexy-as-hell body, and the obvious desire on his face, I was so freaking close to doing something incredibly stupid.

Incredibly. Stupid.

With the capitals.

"I've seen this before," I went on. "We save someone, and they attach themselves like a limpet."

His golden eyes flashed. Good. Or at least, that was what I was telling myself.

"It's a totally normal reaction. I've seen it many times over the years."

Lie.

I mean, I *had* seen it.

But not all that often, especially in Darlington, where nothing really ever happened.

Not that this man needed to know that, especially since I could see the pissed-off creeping into his face.

Good, I thought again.

That was exactly what I needed.

He'd get mad and back off and—

He smiled.

My breath froze in my lungs.

Because it was *that* smile again. The one that made a longing bubble up inside me, made me yearn and ache and wish that the smile could be real and could be for *me*.

Back to Stupid, with that capital S.

His fingers continued moving and he moved closer, his lips to my ear. "I might believe you," he whispered hotly. "If I hadn't wanted you from the moment I saw you kick off your heels."

My breath wheezed out of me. "What?" I breathed.

A dart of a hot, wet tongue, my nerves exploding with sensation.

Then he straightened. "You feel good enough to sit up now?"

I wasn't feeling *anything*—or at least, I wasn't feeling any *pain*. What I *was* feeling was desire and need and trembling thighs and a damp, empty pus—

"I'm good," I said, putting my elbows beneath me and shoving myself up, thanking desire and pain pills for my increased mobility. I should probably be thanking the oxycodone rather than my attraction to Talbot, but I had a feeling that science and the study of drugs binding with pain receptors was actually far less superior to the power of this smiling Hollywood heartthrob.

He slipped his fingers around my arm—the uninjured one—and helped me sit.

"I really am good," I said, knowing I was repeating myself. But it was true for two reasons. First, the pain pills had truly kicked in, and second, I had a feeling this man would be able to play my body like an instrument.

One stroke of his finger on my skin, one hot word whispered in my ear, and I was feeling nothing of my exploits from the night before.

"Here," he murmured, tugging the blankets back and helping me shift my legs so they hung over the edge of the mattress, my bright red toenails barely brushing the plush area rug spread out on the blond-colored floor.

That was when I saw the chair.

Or rather the blanket and pillow sitting in the chair.

Along with his shoes resting beneath the wooden legs.

"You didn't!" I exclaimed.

Golden eyes on mine. "Didn't what?"

I nodded toward the chair. "Tell me, you didn't sleep in that chair all night."

He hesitated, gaze drifting behind him to said chair then back to mine. "Okay, I didn't sleep in that chair *all* night."

It was the emphasis on *all* that got me.

"Talbot!" I poked him in the chest.

He caught my finger. "I like it when you call me Tal better." A nip to the tip, his expression teasing. "Don't worry about where I slept or didn't sleep. Did you want a shower before I make you breakfast?"

"My arm . . ."

"My assistant came by this morning and bought this"—he crossed to the bathroom, brought back a bag—"it's a cast cover, but Dr. Stevens said it'll work fine for this when I spoke to her this morning."

He'd run out?

He'd spoken to the doctor?

Aw. Seriously. Really, really *aw*.

But also, what the fuck? As in, what in the fuck was this man doing? With me? To me? No, *with*—

No. The prepositions in this didn't matter.

What did, however, was the reason behind all of it.

"What are you doing, Tal?" I asked, using the shortened name before I could catch myself.

"How do you mean?"

I just lifted my eyebrows and waited. It was my Cop Look. One my brother had once said should be patented because it was so effective at getting people—including him—to spill their guts. It was also one that I'd perfected because I'd received it so often from my dad before he'd died.

But it didn't appear to have any effect on this man.

He simply wrapped his fingers around my uninjured arm again and tugged me up from the mattress, walking me slowly, but inexorably, across the floor and into the biggest bathroom I'd ever seen in my life.

The. Biggest.

It was like a spa had thrown up in here.

Which probably wasn't a fair assessment because that implied that it wasn't tasteful, and this space was incredibly tasteful. It was just . . . there was a shower and a bath, a sauna, a room off to one side with a door that was open revealing a urinal and toilet.

Yes, a urinal.

I wrinkled my nose then focused on the vanities.

Two huge sinks surrounded by marble and sitting atop ornate cabinets.

Plus, all around, there were baskets of towels, tiny, elegant bottles on the countertops, all matching the color scheme of grays and whites. It was plush. It was gorgeous. It was—

I frowned, turned to face him. "Didn't you say that you were moving?"

He didn't seem taken aback by my abrupt question. "Yes, I am."

"But . . . *why?*"

Talbot stepped a little closer, and I tried to ignore the heat of him as he bent to examine my arm—or well, I realized as I tore my gaze away from the urinal again, he wasn't studying it, but instead removing the bandage.

"Shower?" he asked, unwinding the gauze.

"Yes, but—"

He turned and left the bathroom, returning a few moments later with the cast cover and a fresh pair of sweats and T-shirt, all of which he set on the counter. But he didn't stop by me again, and I definitely wasn't missing his touch on my skin. Nope. I wasn't. No freaking way. I didn't care about that touch as he walked to the shower, turned it on.

Still in that towel.

With most of his gorgeous body on display.

"How often do you work out?" I blurted, staring at the rigid lines of muscle on his back.

He straightened from adjusting the knobs, slowly turning around, and I would have to be blind to miss his raised eyebrows, the surprised look on his face. I was a little near-sighted, but it wasn't enough to save me from my embarrassment of that expression.

From the pleased look creeping into his.

From the slow, hot smile that curved his lips, that flashed a dimple in my direction, that . . .

I spun around, marching toward the cast cover, happy that my muscles were loosening up. My arm barely hurt, and though my knees stung a bit from where the sweats rubbed at the abrasions, I knew I'd be okay and back to normal soon.

Maybe I could even make my theme park visit for the next day.

That lure of churros and soft pretzels in my future took my mind off the critical embarrassment of me asking this man how often he works out.

Who did that?

What kind of *woman* did that?

I might as well be asking, *"You lift, bro?"* God, it was so ridiculous. It was . . . so . . . me.

"I'll work out twice as hard if you keep looking at me like that."

CHAPTER NINE

Talbot

SHE GASPED AND WHIRLED AROUND, her shoulder—thankfully attached to her arm that wasn't hurt—colliding with my chest and knocking me back a step.

I felt the towel around my waist shift and loosen and quickly grabbed it.

But then she spun back, her hands coming up to her cheeks, and took a step as though to run out of the room.

Unfortunately, she'd discounted the too-big sweats.

One long stride had her stumbling, had her falling toward the floor.

I let go of the towel and reached for her, catching one hand, slipping an arm around her waist and stalling her fall. The downside of this?

My towel fell.

Another downside?

I tripped over said towel and stumbled, ass-first onto the cold tile, bringing Tammy down in a heap on top of me. We both grunted. I cursed—because cold fucking tile—and her cheeks went red.

Very red.

Her palms were on my chest.

Her legs in those baggy sweats were straddling my hips.

Her mouth, lush and pink and so damned tempting, parted.

"Wow," she whispered, her hands convulsing.

I bit back a groan.

"Tal?" she asked.

"Hmm?" I was trying very hard to stifle my moans of pleasure, having her over me, her thighs straddling mine, her hands on me. Each of those was chipping away at my control, making it very difficult for me to remember that she was hurt and I couldn't flip her onto her back, slide those sweats down, and get my tongue inside her pussy.

"Do you really like me?" she whispered. "Or is it a pity like? Or a hero complex like? Or a—" She pressed her lips together.

I was still attempting to harbor control.

I was still failing.

Even as I knew I had to say something, say anything, say . . . *anything!*

Get your shit together, Green!

My head finally started working again, and the one above my neck, rather than the one positioned so gloriously between her thighs. "I like you, sweetheart. I liked you even before you came to my rescue." I lifted my hand, cupped her jaw. "And this is definitely not a pity erection." I curled up, snaking an arm around her waist and drawing her closer to me. "This is an I-want-the-sexy-woman-on-top-of-me erection, and I want her quite desperately."

Her mouth parted, her breath coating mine.

"Oh," she whispered.

I tucked the strands of honey-blond hair behind her ear. "Yeah, *oh.*"

Hazel eyes changing color, swirling with gray and green and amber.

Then . . .

She bent and pressed her lips to mine.

At first, I couldn't move, I was so stunned. Her lips were surprisingly soft, especially considering the night before this woman had single-handedly taken down a man six inches taller and probably fifty pounds heavier than her with ease.

And considering the chip she wore on her shoulder.

Most women melted at the first smile I tossed their way, and that wasn't ego talking. That was plain truth and just a product of the world I lived it. I could give them something—notoriety, a job, connections they could exploit.

That was my reality.

This—a woman who didn't melt at a flash of my dimple, who didn't care that I was in movies, who couldn't give two shits who my friends were—was the most incredible thing I'd experienced in a long time, and I'd been lucky enough to experience a lot of incredible things in the last few years.

My childhood had been shit.

The world knew it.

Many people had tried to exploit it.

But not Tammy. She didn't know. She wasn't trying to use me.

She'd *saved* me.

And then had stared at my body like it was a temptation she was desperate for, her hands on my skin, and now her lips against mine.

It was . . . nothing and everything and too much and not enough. It was nothing because it felt like this was a kiss she had given me a million times before. There wasn't any learning, any fumbling my-nose-goes-this-way, yours-goes-that-way delays. Our teeth didn't click. Our mouths didn't miss. This was nothing extraordinary. And yet, it was also the most incredible thing I'd ever experienced. That familiarity, that sense of being home and completely comfortable was tangled with desire, with need, with heat. Her tongue wasn't shy. It slipped between my lips, stroked alongside mine, coaxing it into action. Her hands drifted up to my shoulders, the short bite of her nails the sweetest pain.

But it wasn't enough because those hands didn't move, other than to knead at the muscles on either side of my neck. I didn't band my arms around her and yank her lithe body against mine, didn't flip us and stroke home, plunging into her heat and taking us both into oblivion. And it was too much. Because I'd had this sense of the world shifting since the night before in the garden, an abrupt jar of my place on this planet, the axis tilted to the side, my normal orbit adjusted without warning, and this kiss increased that feeling.

I felt both completely changed and also completely myself.

The juxtaposition was intense.

A soft moan slid up her throat, vibrated across my tongue, filled my mouth with the sweet taste of her pleasure, and then I wasn't trying to quantify this moment. I was just *in the moment*.

I threaded my fingers into her hair, tilted her head, slanting our lips, deepening the contact, tasting every inch of her mouth as the golden locks tickled the back of my hand, made me wish I was feeling it drag across my chest, down my stomach, drift over my cock as she took me deep. My other palm slid down her back, not stopping until I was cupping the delicious, curved globes, her moan as I stroked and massaged them, making red edge into the corners of my eyes.

She bucked, thighs widening, pressing tighter against me.

My towel was long gone, but her sweats were in place, a frustrating barrier that I was desperate to get rid of.

I slipped my hand under the waistband on her back, felt the velvet roughness of the lace encircling her hips, the band dipping down between her cheeks. I followed those lines, tracing every inch of her ass before shifting my fingers around to the front of her, moving it down, sliding into damp heat.

She gasped, bucked again, and fuck, that felt good.

I slid a little deeper, circling the bundle of nerves, tracing light patterns over her labia, making her mouth break away from mine, her head fall back, her eyes slide closed. "Tal," she whispered. "I—"

"Should I stop?" I murmured, kissing my way up her throat until I reached her ear, my tongue darting out to taste the sensitive spot just behind it.

Stillness.

And I felt an answering motionless enter my body, freeze my every cell and nerve in place.

Then she pulled back slightly, and I prepared myself for her to pull out of my embrace, to find her feet. Her hazel eyes connected with mine, held, and I found myself immobile for a completely different reason as the moment stretched and she was silent in my arms, the only noise the sound of our rapid breathing and the shower running in the background.

No words. No sense of what was going through that mind of hers.

Her lips parted, her tongue dipping out to taste the bottom one. My cock twitched, but I didn't consciously move a muscle, not when it felt as though my new orbit hinged on what she decided in this moment.

Breath slipped free, coating my skin with humid warmth, mixing with the steam of the shower, heat seeping into every inch of me.

That heat turned into an inferno when she whispered, "No."

A match in dry tinder. A forest bursting into flames from multiple strikes of lightning. Nothing but leaves and sticks and grass and trees, but then one instance and . . . flames along every inch of the foreseeable landscape.

"No," she said again, fanning those flames, throwing gasoline on the fire. "I don't want you to stop."

And then she kissed me again.

Fuck, that was good.

Our lips and tongues dueled, but this time her hands didn't stay on my shoulders. They slid up and down my torso, fingernails grazing my nipples, shooting pleasure down my spine, drifting lower . . . and encircling my cock.

Now *my* head dropped back, my hips lurched up, and my dick went even harder.

"I want you," she whispered, tugging her mouth free, the words soft puffs against my throat. "I shouldn't want you. It's dangerous and stupid, but"—her tongue darted out—"I want you anyway. Will you . . ." Her eyes came up. "Will you have me?"

Pink dusting her cheekbones, desire in the depths of her gaze.

But also . . . courage. So much courage inside this woman, to ask for what she wanted, to not hide her need. I didn't like the dangerous and stupid tag—though after last night I couldn't deny the former. But the wanting me, the having her. *Those* I could work with.

When I didn't immediately answer, the pink deepened, her stare drifted away.

"Yes, Hazel Eyes," I murmured, using one hand to cup her jaw, to tilt her head back toward mine. "Yes, I'll have you." I ran my thumb back and forth over her skin, loving that she shivered at my touch. "As long as you're sure that the pills haven't gone to your head, that you won't regret this later."

Her eyes were lucid, but I had to be sure. I didn't want her to look back and hate herself or me for doing this.

Shadows in her eyes. Her hand lifting to cover mine. "I have lots of regrets," she whispered. "But I can promise you this won't be one of them." A beat as she swallowed, her chin lifting. "So, will you take me, Tal? Will you have me?"

Forever.

I'd have her forever, take her forever, *keep* her forever.

My lips found hers, tasting deeply as I rose to my feet, as I moved us into the bedroom and back across the space. I set her on the mattress, pausing only to tug off the overly large sweats, to ease the shirt over her head.

Black lace.

No bra.

And fuck but her breasts were all that I'd imagined. Lush handfuls, the pink nipples pouty and demanding to be kissed. Her body was gently curved, the evidence of her job in every muscle. Strong arms, shoulders, and legs, a slender waist, hips a man could hold on to.

"Tal," she whispered, crossing her arms beneath her breasts, the injury on her arm visible and infuriating.

Hurt because of me.

Hurt that was my fault.

But I was going to make her feel good.

I reached into the nightstand, extracted a condom, and set it on the wood. Then I turned my full attention to this woman, to discovering what gave her pleasure. I climbed onto the mattress, nudged her legs wide, and I kissed her, careful to brace my weight with one hand.

The other slid down her side, cupped her breast, capturing one beaded nipple between thumb and forefinger.

She moaned, her head thrown back, her hips bucking against mine. "Please."

It was a whispered plea, her uninjured arm lifting, fingers threading into my hair and tugging my head down to her breast, and I'll admit that I got lost there for a minute. For . . . much longer than a minute as I lavished her breasts with my tongue, with my teeth, with my lips. I nipped at the delicate undersides, sucked the sensitive tips deep, traced the soft skin with my tongue.

A soft sheen of sweat coated her body, kissing the tip of my tongue with salt as I dragged it lower, across her torso, delving into the soft dip of her navel, the creases on either side of her pelvis.

Then along the folds of her labia, nuzzling into the damp heat, using my lips against hers so I could taste her sweet musk. Her fingers, still in my hair, convulsed, drawing me nearer, and

I focused on the spot that had made her react, filing away what made her squirm, what made more of those soft, breathy moans emerge, what had her head tossing back again, her hips jerking and grinding against my mouth.

"Tal—"

Her voice changed, hitched, her skin glistening in the sunlight, making me so damned glad that I hadn't closed the blinds, so fucking thankful that I could see every expression on her face, every line of her body. The play of desire through her eyes, the way her lips deepened to a dusky pink, the cords of her neck standing out in sharp relief. Her breasts heaving in time to her breath, her rib cage expanding and contracting, her thighs wrapped tight around me.

And then she froze.

And then she made that hitched sound again, and I knew she was there, that she was ready to explode, that I just needed to nudge her over the precipice.

I pressed the flat of my tongue to her clit, slipped another finger inside, and I put every single trick I'd garnered over the years, everything I'd learned about her body over the last minutes to good use.

To good benefit.

Because her breathing sped up, the movement of her hips increased, her moans rose in volume, and then . . . she crumpled.

Her moans softened. Her thighs went limp. Her fingers loosened their grip.

I slowed my strokes, slipped my fingers free, gently dragged my lips from her, brushing them light over either thigh, pressing a light kiss to each before moving up her body and lying on her uninjured side.

"You're fucking beautiful," I murmured, stroking my thumb over the swathe of pink on her cheeks.

She tilted her head to look at me, and I couldn't read what was in her eyes. But when she spoke, her words were light.

They were also sexy as hell, and complete confidence, just a glimpse of that chip on her shoulder—in the form of one arched brow. "Is there a reason you're not inside me yet?"

My cock twitched. But—

"Yeah, about that," I began.

Her expression changed, and I hated that there was a glimpse of embarrassment in her eyes before they darted away, and she started to sit up. That sliver of insecurity had me quickly cupping her cheeks.

"Hey, that's—"

"It's okay," she said, propping herself on one elbow and pushing up. "I get it." A chuckle that sounded completely different from the few natural ones I'd managed to coax from her sounded completely wrong.

"You don't get it." I shifted my hips close, letting her feel the hard length of my cock. "I want you, baby," I murmured. "Certainly more than any other woman I've ever wanted"—she scoffed—"It's true. I just . . . I'm not convinced that you won't regret doing this when not under the influence of narcotics. And you were hurting, baby. I don't want you to be in more pain because of me. I—"

One swift move, and I found myself on my back, beautiful, naked woman crawling on top of me, her fingers circling my cock.

CHAPTER TEN

Tammy

I PROBABLY SHOULD BE GETTING up, running from the room, yanking that T-shirt and sweats back on.

I certainly shouldn't be reaching for the condom, tearing it open with my teeth, rolling it down the length of his hard cock.

I definitely shouldn't be ignoring the protesting stitches on my upper arm as I positioned him between my thighs, dropped down enough to take the tip of his erection inside.

But . . . it had been so long.

I wanted this man, my need bordering on desperately wanting him. He was sweet and he'd slept in the chair next to me, watching over me (in a non-creepy way—or at least, that was how I was taking it). He'd called in a doctor to take care of me. He'd helped me with the pain pills and getting changed and to the bathroom. Sweet. Lovely. So freaking out of my league.

But for the moment, he was with me.

He was looking hotly at me, at my body, at my face like I was beautiful and feminine, seeing my strength as an asset instead of as something that took away.

And his cock was hard for me.

I knew this couldn't last; fairy tales didn't come in the form of Hollywood hunks falling for small-town female police officers. Those spheres didn't cross. Except . . . for today, they did. Today I could have that fantasy, soak up the kind, nice man, enjoy the hard lines of his muscles, the scrape of his stubble, his talented fingers and tongue.

I could enjoy his hard cock inside me.

And that would be enough.

Because I'd have lived out a fantasy.

I paused, my hips desperate to slide down, to take him deeper, but just as he'd needed to confirm I was with him, I needed to do the same.

I could live out my fantasy, but only if I knew that he was with me in it.

"Tal?" I whispered, statue still, the blunt head of him stretching me wide, promising more pleasure if I . . . just . . . sank . . . lower.

His eyes were liquid metal.

Then his hands came to my waist and slowly, inexorably tugged me down the length of his erection.

And I know that people always said that their man had a big dick, that romance heroes were built like freaking elephants, that every dude had a nine-inch cock. But I'd been with more than a handful of men (cough, nineteen and Talbot would make twenty), and maybe that number made me a bit of a slut, but my point was that I'd been with enough men to know that *this* cock was special. It stretched me wide, wide enough that I cursed, the slight burn of pain mingling with the pleasure of being filled. I know he was bigger at this angle, but it wasn't just the angle. The man had a glorious cock.

A *magical* cock.

A magical cock? Dear lord. I stifled a giggle.

Fingers touching my mouth, tracing a curve I hadn't even known was there. "What?" he murmured.

I had to admit that the slight strain in his voice made my smile tip up further.

"What?" he asked again.

I shook my head, nibbling at the corner of my mouth.

His thumb pressed against my bottom lip, dragging it out from beneath my teeth. "Tammy," he warned.

"Talbot," I countered, having adjusted to him and testing out shifting my hips, grinding down. Oh, sweet baby Jesus, that felt good . . . no it felt great, pleasure radiating throughout my center, splintering along my limbs, making everything from my toes to my tongue tingle. "Shut up," I moaned. "And let's just fuck."

He cursed, and then he was sitting up, one arm banding around my waist, pressing us tighter together. I gasped, the angle of him inside me even deeper, even *better*.

"What?" he murmured again, and this time it was accompanied by a nip against my lips.

More zinging.

More pleasure.

His wide palm covered one of my cheeks, tilting my ass so I hit just the right spot. My head fell back, vision blearily recognizing the wooden bed frame overhead. Teeth on my throat, my pussy tightening around him, making us both groan. But aside from that tilting, he held me in place, held me deep.

Even though I was growing wetter by the moment, getting more and more desperate to move, *he held me still.*

"Tell me," he demanded.

My vision blurred further, I could feel an orgasm coiling in my abdomen, just from him being in and in deep, just from this man's—

"You have a magical cock," I blurted.

He did an impression of a statue, frozen and stiff, and as mortification tangled with desire, he flipped me over to my back with hardly a jostle—one second I was on top of him, the next I was cushioned on the mattress, his lips curving, his eyes filled with desire and humor.

"Well then," he murmured, humor in his tone as his lips came to my ear. "Let me put this magical cock to work."

He began moving, not slow and inching, not teasing and gentle, but firm, deep strokes that had my hips lifting up from the bed, rising to meet his thrusts, that coiling orgasm spiraling tighter, growing tauter, readying for implosion.

His mouth was on mine then on my throat, my collarbones, one nipple and then the other, and then the orgasm wasn't just in my abdomen.

It was exploding outward, filling my entire body with pleasure, sending my muscles contracting, setting my nerves on fire, and then leaving me limp and satiated, the aftereffects of all that bliss sparkling through me as Tal stroked deeper once, twice, three times more, his head dropping to my shoulder as his own orgasm tugged him down. He collapsed on top of me. Though collapsed wasn't quite the right word. He gave me his weight, hips settling on mine, his torso pressed to mine, but one elbow was propped near my shoulder, making sure he didn't squash me, didn't crush my injured arm.

And that small bit of care undid me.

I was falling headfirst down a dangerous slope, longing for a fantasy that could never actually be reality.

As though he sensed that panic, that despair creeping in— even though I told myself to just enjoy the good time, to appreciate the pair of glorious orgasms and not want for anything more, even more of that fantasy—Talbot pushed up, his pupils still dilated, his forehead sheened with sweat, his damp hair skewed in every direction. "What is it?" he asked, fingers coming to my cheek. "Did I hurt you?"

"No," I said quickly.

"Then what?" His thumb swept under each eye, not to wipe away tears because I wasn't weak enough to give in to them at this moment, even though misery at my stupidity was becoming rampant. I'd opened Pandora's box, letting hope escape. I'd peeked inside the treasure chest and found it empty —or perhaps filled with jewels and gold I couldn't carry home. I'd tasted ambrosia but would never again be able to savor the food of the gods.

Later, I'd pick up a sad-ass book. I'd let myself cry about the characters, rid myself of this knot, even while trying to convince the universe that the tears weren't about me at all. I was just wrapped up in the story.

I'd done it time and again.

Plenty of grief, plenty of heartbreak.

Plenty of techniques to pretend I had neither.

"That was good," I said, not letting him coax another confession out of me. *Magical cock* was bad enough. He didn't need to know about my *sad-ass* childhood, nor the various sad-ass things of my adulthood.

Hell, no one knew everything about all that happened.

Not Maggie. Though she knew parts.

The rest of it, I held closer, buried deeper. Because it was the only way I knew how to survive.

"Tammy," he warned in that delicious raspy voice.

But I wasn't weak. I wouldn't give into that sexy order. Even though I *really* wanted to, had really enjoyed where it had taken me in the last thirty minutes.

I wound my arms around his shoulders, brought his mouth down to mine. "You do have a magical cock," I murmured, and then I kissed him, wondering if I could distract him long enough to escape, how I could interrupt his inquisition and don some armor to protect myself from the man and my fantasies and my weak, desperate heart.

Footsteps.

I didn't register them at first.

Not until they were coming closer. *Closer.*

I tore my lips free, breathing heavily, trying to listen over the sound of my pulse thrumming in my eardrums.

Talbot was in no better shape. His breaths puffed against my mouth as he said, "Tell me—"

And then I got my interruption.

Only . . . I wasn't able to escape as Maggie strode into the bedroom. "Why the fuck didn't you call me—*oh my God!*"

CHAPTER ELEVEN

Talbot

I WHIPPED my head over my shoulder at the gasp, unwittingly exposing Tammy to Maggie's gaze.

"Tammy?" she breathed then immediately clamped her hands over her eyes before spinning around and knocking into the doorframe as she fumbled her way out of the bedroom. "Oh, son of a paparazzo."

A moment later, her arm reappeared, but not her body, as that almost disembodied limb reached for the knob, dragging the door shut.

Click.

Yeah, the first thing I could think was, *Oh, son of a paparazzo.*

Yeah, I'd stolen it from Maggie.

Yeah, it was apropos.

Tammy was shoving at my chest, and I pulled out, my cock still rock-hard. Despite the orgasm, it wasn't nearly satisfied. *I* wasn't nearly satisfied, especially when her lips formed a small little "O" as I left her body. Then she shoved up off the bed, digging her hands into her hair, a soft moan leaving her mouth.

But not one of the soft, *sexy* moans she'd been making just a few minutes before.

No, this one was a soft sigh of misery.

"Hey," I said, coming up next to her.

Another groan.

"Are you in pain?"

"Pain of embarrassment, maybe," she muttered, finally lifting her hands from her face and looking up at me. "How much did she see?"

"Would it make you feel better if I told you it was more of me than you?"

Her face screwed up. "No, in fact, it wouldn't." She was quiet for a beat. "Okay, yes, it would." Hazel eyes on mine. "My childhood bestie didn't see my hoohaw?"

My lips twitched.

She swatted me.

"It's not so bad," I said. "It's not the first time—"

Her fingers pressed to my lips. "I'm gonna stop you right there."

I peeled her fingers free. "I was going to say, *It's not the first time Maggie has seen me naked.*"

"I *said*, I don't want to know."

"However," I said, being purposefully blithe as I continued, "This is the first time she's caught me with a woman."

"I'm so happy to be the first," she muttered.

"My point is that there haven't *been* any other women."

"Pft." She pushed to her feet. "Okay, sure."

I stood, too. "Sweetheart."

"So *not* your sweetheart," she snapped.

God, I liked her fire. But also, I could give some back of my own. "I was inside you all of two minutes ago." Her cheeks went pink. "So obviously, you're something to me."

"A quick fuck?"

My temper peaked, and I found myself whirling to face her, fury in my voice. "You're more than that."

Another "Pft." Her lips pressing flat. "We met all of yesterday. Oh, and also, you being allowed inside my body doesn't link us together in any way."

The hell it didn't.

The sex had been fan-fucking-tastic, but it wasn't just a fucking orgasm. There was more here, something worth exploring, and I'd felt it the moment she'd confronted me in the garden.

But she was still talking. "And it certainly doesn't obligate me to your continued presence."

No, it didn't.

Of course, it didn't.

Except . . . every cell in my body rebelled with the thought of just letting her walk out of my life.

I took her hand. "You saved me."

A scoff, drawing her hand away. "More hero-worship bullshit."

"Tammy," I said.

Her teeth closed with an audible *click,* and she yanked the blanket off the bed, wrapping it around her. "I'd take the warning out of your tone if I were you."

My temper was still frayed, growing even more so by the moment, by this woman's resistance to admitting that there was something between us, even if that *something* was just a slender thread of connection, a green bud in the first stages of unfurling. But I'd had plenty of experiences in my life dealing with recalcitrant actors, and certainly a lot of experience with stubborn ass co-stars.

Enough that I could keep my temper.

Barely.

But I could still keep hold of it.

And the Oscar goes to . . .

"Tammy," I said, making doubly sure that there wasn't any attitude or warning in my voice. In fact, I made sure that my tone was completely and absolutely even with no trace of order or anger. "Why don't you take that shower? I'll go handle Maggie."

Her lips pressed flat, which was an absolute crime against humanity. But her eyes told me that she was going to protest, just because protesting would mean that she didn't have to agree with me.

"Come on," I cajoled lightly. "I'm sure you want to feel clean."

I hustled to the bathroom to retrieve the waterproof cover, pausing only to grab my towel and wrap it around my waist. I'd deal with the condom later.

"See?" I said, moving back to her and holding it up, waving it around like a flag. "I'll help you get it on and leave you to get settled and—"

Something flashed across her eyes.

My words came faster. "I won't look, I promise, I'll just—"

Fingers on my arm.

"Okay."

"And a shower will—" I broke off, turned to look at her. "You're agreeing with me?"

There was still something almost fragile about her, as though pressure in the wrong spot might shatter her into pieces. But then she smiled, and I saw that flash again, only this time it was definitely tinged with amusement. Not a lot of it, as her tone was still a little bit sharp, but at least enough to take the sting out. "Can you spend at least *one* moment not arguing with me?" A beat. "Just one?"

I shut up, just nodded in response, and slipped the cover up and over her arm. "Okay?" I asked, smoothing the edge to make sure it would keep her arm dry.

"Yup."

She brushed past me, taking the blanket with her.

I followed, moving into the bathroom and immediately pulling out several fresh towels, a new toothbrush, and my toothpaste. Then, inspiration striking, I dug in my linen cabinet and pulled out a gift bag from an event I'd gone to the week before. Usually, I passed, but this one had been pressed into my hand as I'd left the party, and I hadn't been able to demur. Today, however, it came in handy. I set it on the counter and pulled out the hair and body products. "Probably not your brand," I said. "But they've got to be better than my stuff." I nodded at the counter, where I had some deodorant, face wash, and other stuff. "Feel free to use mine, though, if you'd prefer."

She swallowed, was quiet for a long time. "Okay," she whispered. "Thanks."

I nodded, slipped into the toilet room to finally deal with the condom, then stopped back by the sink to quickly wash my hands. The shower was still on, filling the room with sticky, humid air. I flicked on the fan, knowing that I was probably singlehandedly responsible for California's drought that day but unable to regret what had just happened with this woman.

Hell, regret was the absolute *last* thing on my mind.

That had been incredible. *She* had been incredible.

"I'll go take care of Maggie," I said, unable to stop myself from cupping her cheek, from feeling some part of her skin against mine. "You take your time in here. Holler if you need anything."

I watched her throat work as she swallowed then smiled gently when she nodded.

It was harder to force my hand to drop, to make my feet carry me back, carry me away from her and out the door of the bathroom, across to my closet to get some clothes on—no need to scar Maggie twice in one day.

And then I had to keep forcing them to move out into the hall, and then to the kitchen, where my lovely, beautiful, scowling publicist was standing next to the island, her arms crossed, her toe tapping on the ground, as I closed the distance between us.

One finger poked into my chest. Hard.

"What in the *fuck* do you think you're doing, Talbot Green?"

CHAPTER TWELVE

Tammy

FOR FUCK'S SAKE.

I was waffling more than a . . . well, a waffle.

One second, I was critically embarrassed, ready to run (not screaming) from this house and get the fuck back to my own life, one that was far, far away from all things Talbot Green related.

And the next—

"What, Tammy?" I muttered, shampooing my hair with a product that looked like it would cost more than my car—and that was just the sample size. "Because the truth is that you got all squishy and happy, and your spine turned to Jell-O when the man got a little flustered." I shoved my hair into the stream. "Because he wanted to take care of you."

Look, I got it, okay?

That was my weak spot. I'd always been the one to do the caring, and when someone wanted to look out for me for a change (something that never happened—okay, something that had perhaps happened a half-dozen times, all courtesy of my asshole ex-husband), I went all gooey inside.

Stupid, huh?

More capital S.

Sighing, knowing it was only a matter of time before I headed over the cliff to absolute heartbreak, I decided that I was just going back to that fantasy.

Talbot was guy number twenty.

And it had been fabulous.

Now, I was ready to exit Stage Right.

"Exactly, Tam," I said, smoothing some luxurious conditioner into my hair. It felt like the expensive stuff my hairdresser used on my bi-annual appointments, the stuff I never splurged for because I spent ninety percent of my life with my hair wrestled back into a ponytail or bun, and the other ten letting it air dry straight out of the shower. It was drugstore shampoo and conditioner, all the way, no matter how much she tried to convince me to treat my hair to something special.

I didn't even treat myself with something special.

Why would I binge on my hair?

"Maybe I should steal the container," I muttered. "Ferret it into my pocket and slip out the front door with it."

I wouldn't do that. Of course, I wouldn't (maybe). But I wanted to (definitely). No, no. I wouldn't. It would be wrong, and Talbot had been nice, and even though I wanted to jump on the man like a monkey, to beg for another round of orgasms, I knew that I wouldn't survive a second interlude.

The man had already reduced me to goo almost effortlessly.

"I thought that stealing and illicit drugs are right up there together on the list of bad things bad guys do."

I froze, having been almost mesmerized by the feel of my ends after I'd rinsed out the conditioner. They were softer than I'd ever felt before, and maybe my hairdresser wasn't just trying to hawk me expensive product after all.

Talbot's voice was . . . a warm blanket, the sunshine coating my skin on a warm summer day. It was—*hell*, it was amused and laced with a little bit of heat, and it was the absolute sexiest thing I'd ever heard. It was also something that I shouldn't be hearing.

Because the man had promised he wouldn't look.

"You said you wouldn't," I exclaimed.

"Tammy—"

"How typical," I muttered, both to remind myself that this was my common experience with men—that they didn't keep their commitments—"of a man to not follow through." Also, maybe I wanted to push him away. Just a little bit. No, I wanted to push him so far that he realized now what he would realize eventually.

That he didn't have any interest in sticking by one Tammy Conners.

It was as simple as that.

Which was to say, it wasn't simple at all.

Such an idiot. Why had I decided to embrace the fantasy?

Stupid. Capital S.

"Tammy."

"Promises are so easy to make," I grumbled, shutting off the water and cracking the door to the steam shower I really didn't want to get out of. I hadn't had a chance to play with the body wash, and it had actual gold flakes in it. *Gold flakes!*

"Tam—"

I yanked a towel off the heated rack, wrapped it around my head, which I had to say was a fair shade more difficult with the rubber-plastic-sleeve thing around my arm. But I managed, just like I managed to continue my tirade.

Inside, I knew I was being ridiculous, that it was his house.

That it wasn't like he hadn't just seen all I had to offer a bare half hour ago.

But deeper inside, I was grasping onto every straw that would make it so the man stopped being nice and sweet and funny and kind and an excellent giver of double orgasms—a fate that most men in my collection of twenty had definitely not been able to achieve.

"Look at me," he snapped, firmly enough that my gaze drifted from the fluffy white towel over to the man in question. "Tammy," he growled. "Are you looking?"

I was looking.

Probably very confused.

Because Talbot was in the bathroom, but his back was toward the shower stall. He'd pulled on faded jeans that clung to a truly glorious ass and a tight heather red T-shirt that seemed to kiss each muscled inch of his back. His hair was still a mess from my fingers tossing the shower-damp locks this way and that during our escapades, and I felt an actual itch in my fingertips to straighten it.

Or perhaps, to mess it up all over again.

"Tam—"

"I'm looking," I wheezed out, unable to believe I could still want this man so much after I'd had him.

That wasn't usually the case with me.

Typically, I was searching for more feeling, more sensation, for something to cling on to.

That clearly wasn't a probably when it came to Talbot.

"Good," he said. "Are you decent?"

I'd wrapped a towel around myself during my muttering. "Yeah," I whispered.

"Good," he said again, spinning to face me. "Clothes," he said, plunking down the bundle in his arms onto the counter. "Hairbrush," he added, setting it on the stack. "Courtesy of another gift bag. Do you want me to help you take off the cover?"

Clipped words.

Distance, I'd wanted.

And fuck me, distance I didn't.

I nearly groaned out loud, because seriously, what in the fuck was the matter with me? Why was I tormenting myself? Why was I taking my own past and insecurities out on Talbot when he'd only ever been nice to me?

"Tammy?" he asked again, his tone still chill.

I was cursing myself every which way, so I didn't have the energy to summon words.

In their place, I just nodded.

He crossed to me, long legs eating up the large space in mere heartbeats, and then his body was next to mine, the spicy, male scent of him filling the air, reminding my nerves, my lips, my nipples, my pussy of exactly how much it had liked being this close to him.

But, if he noticed my reaction, he didn't comment on it.

Instead, his hand lifted, fingers gentle on my skin as he eased the cover past the stitches on the outside of my arm, down its length, and then off.

My breath froze in my lungs when he bent close, pressed his lips to the red marks encircling my biceps, where the cover had been tight to my skin.

Then he straightened, and those golden eyes locked with mine. "For the record," he said, the words sharp and scalding over my body like a lash from a whip, "I'm not like other men." That, I knew. That, I could have told him. But any words died on my tongue, because the man came closer, his lips a millimeter from mine. "I keep my fucking promises."

With that, he was gone.

And I was left staring at his back, knowing that I was absolutely, irrevocably sunk.

CHAPTER THIRTEEN

Talbot

I'D LEFT a flabbergasted Maggie back in the kitchen after she'd followed me around my house as I'd searched for another gift bag I'd shoved in some closet or another—before finding it in a cupboard above the washing machine.

I'd known it was somewhere around, knew that Tammy's hair was too long and thick for my comb to be of any use, so I'd ignored Maggie's words as I'd searched.

I'd ignored them long enough that her snapped out rebukes and sighs had evened out, until she'd gone absolutely quiet as she'd followed me, until she'd finally burst out, "What are you doing?" just as I'd entered the laundry room.

"Looking for something," had been my response.

Which had led to more grumbling, more rebukes.

But by then, I'd found the brush and had disappeared back into the bathroom.

Now, however, I didn't have any bags to be searching for, any products to unearth. It was just me and my publicist, who was, without a doubt, the person who knew me best in the entire world.

Her arms were still crossed, but her toe wasn't tapping, which was why I knew that the worst of the storm of her temper had passed.

Maggie didn't get mad often—fuck, I hadn't even realized she'd *had* a temper until we'd worked together over a year. I'd just gotten my quote-unquote big break, and some gossip columnist had done some digging into my past. My juvenile case had been sealed, and I'd changed my name.

But no data in this world was ever safe, and he'd connected the dots.

The story had blown up in the absolute worst way.

I hadn't been prepared for the attention, hadn't been ready to face those memories. I'd had no security, no system, no backup.

Except Maggie.

Who was looking at me with disappointment in her eyes.

Ouch. That fucking hurt.

I needed to be doing something. Right now, I needed to find something to do with my hands, something that wasn't looking at my friend, who was looking at *me* like I'd let her down in the absolute worst way.

Food.

Yes.

I was hungry. Tammy would be hungry, too. And she needed to eat in order to not get an upset stomach with her antibiotics and painkillers.

Dr. Stevens had said so.

And food was something I could make happen.

I crossed to the fridge, started pulling out ingredients for omelets. It was still early, definitely early enough for brunch, and omelets were brunch.

"Do you know if Tammy likes onions?" I asked, grabbing a pack of bacon, along with several peppers from the drawers. I glanced at the bacon, realized something else. "Is she a vegetarian?"

I'd been too busy with other things at the party the night before to see if she'd eaten something, and then she'd left, and I'd followed her—

So, yeah, I didn't know if she actually ate bacon.

Or eggs. Or peppers, onions, and cheese.

Quiet for a long, long moment before she finally answered.

"She's not a vegetarian," Mags said. "And she's one of the most easygoing people I know when it comes to food. She always says, so long as it's not mooing, she'll eat it."

That made me chuckle.

Because it was such a Tammy thing to say.

Then I bent and grabbed a bowl from the cupboard, began cracking eggs and frying up bacon.

Maybe the smell of the latter would lure her from the bedroom.

Or maybe I was slowly losing my mind, the encounter the previous night the final straw.

Also, yay for such happy thoughts before the sun was even at its highest point in the sky.

"You want one?" I asked Maggie, tossing her a glance over my shoulder.

Her mouth twisted, curving up to one side the way it always did when she was displeased with me but wouldn't actually voice that displeasure until later.

Fine by me, I'd take the reprieve when and where I could find it.

"You want the works?"

More mouth twisting, paired with a begrudging nod, but she crossed to the cupboard where I kept the plates and pulled out three. Then she moved to the coffee maker my interior designer had included in the kitchen, one that I'd never used, and began brewing up a pot.

"I know you and I don't drink it," she said, retrieving a mug, "but Tammy needs her sludge to keep her mind functioning." A beat. "And I'm guessing she's going to need it, considering the storm that's about to blindside her."

I flipped the bacon, turned to face her. "What are you talking about?"

"Have you seen the news?"

"No, I was too busy." I shrugged, turned back, thinking this story was the same as any other. It would be front page. It would be blasted around for a few days, but then it would blow over as something much more interesting happened.

"Too busy having sex with my childhood friend," she muttered, just barely audible over the hissing and groaning of the coffee pot.

Biting back a sigh, I turned to face her. "What is between Tammy and me is between Tammy and me. Neither of us have to explain ourselves," I said. "We're both fucking adults, and what happens is our business."

A long pause, then, "You're right, of course."

I nodded, focused on the bacon.

"Of course," Maggie said, "you're also wrong, very, very wrong. This is everywhere, Tal."

I shrugged. "It's always everywhere," I said. "It'll be bad for a bit, and it'll roll over."

Silence then, "Where's your phone?"

"Why?" I asked, flipping the bacon.

"Phone, Tal."

I pointed to the counter on the opposite side of the room, where I'd plugged it in the night before.

She moved to it, muttering, "That's why you didn't pick up when I called."

To which I replied, "In fairness to me, I did try to reach you last night."

To which *she* replied, "In text message, which I didn't get until this freaking morning.

To which *I* replied, "I didn't want to ruin your party."

Which made her sigh and cross to me, wrapping her arms

around my waist and hugging me tight. "You stubborn, wonderful man. I really do love you." A sigh. "You're in the absolute shit," she said. "But I really, truly do love you." Then she swiped her finger across the screen—because obviously, she knew my passcode after all these years—and began tapping away. After a moment, she held it up so I could see the screen.

She'd pulled up the security cameras for the front of my house, and the view made me wince. "Aw, fuck. The neighbors are going to hate me."

A nod. "They're all the way down to Murrieta. Most have their cars positioned on the side of the road, leaving the street mostly clear as they clustered by your front gate, but some are double-parked. I had to curse, meander, and snail's pace my way up here."

"Shit," I muttered.

"The police have already arrived to clear out the double-parkers," she said. "I called them right when I saw the tangle, and they'll act quickly considering it's blocking emergency access. But the group out front of the gate isn't going anywhere anytime soon."

That was to be expected.

"Also, I called the security company. They've staffed extra bodies instead of the usual pair of patrols. Already, they've had to remove three men with long range cameras from around the property, including one in the back yard."

My breath caught.

I'd left the blinds open. My bedroom looked out into the back yard.

Fuck, had they—

Her hand covered mine. "This was earlier this morning, much earlier when I couldn't reach you, so I called them. They reported you were sleeping when they caught the men and that they'd already cleared them out from near the pool area. They also erected a backdrop just beyond all the privacy foliage on the back of the house, just as another layer against prying eyes." She handed me my phone. "The report is in your email."

I released the breath I hadn't even known I'd been holding. "Shit, Mags," I whispered, finally starting to grasp that this was bigger.

"It'll be okay."

"You have to say that," I muttered, pulling the bacon off, and needing to keep my hands busy, I began chopping ingredients while I gave the bacon time to drain. "It's your job."

"That's true."

I snorted.

She placed her hand on my back. "She's fine. You're fine. We'll sort this out."

Not feeling much better, I nodded. It would always feel like this—like the end of the world, like it was the worst thing to happen, like a huge tsunami was cresting my direction and it would swallow me under.

"Fucking paparazzi," I muttered.

"They are a little annoying when they're parked outside your front gate."

I muttered and cursed some more.

A nudge on my back. "Good thing you're moving."

I snorted again, but this time it was paired with a chuckle, with an absurd sense of humor. Nothing about this was funny, and yet, what else could I do but find that note of comedy in it? "Property values have to go up. A major event happened out front."

Mags' lips twitched. "If only your real estate agent had my PR skills."

"If only," I said, grating some cheese. "If she did, I'd probably get double over asking."

"Isn't that the truth?" She made a grab for the block of cheese. "Go back to cracking eggs. I think we're going to need all our strength to come up with a plan to handle this."

I relinquished the block and grater, took up the eggs again, whisking them until they were fluffy—also chef school for a movie role had seriously helped me in this department. "Don't you already have a plan?" I asked, ladling some of the prepared eggs into the pan.

An edgy silence.

"What?"

"Sometimes I don't have it all figured out."

My stomach sank, and I turned to face her. "Wh—" I cut the question off. "Oh, man, you're evil."

She patted my arm, topped the eggs in the pan with some cheese, prompting me to get to work with the peppers, onions, and bacon. "I just don't want you to feel left out, is all. Sometimes you men like to be involved with all the plotting."

"Hilarious," I muttered.

"Aaron seems to think so."

"*Aaron* is getting laid on a regular basis," I grumbled. "It's rotted his brain."

"Speaking of getting laid . . ." She trailed off, not leaving any question that she wanted me to finish that statement.

"Do I need to circle back to Tammy and my business is Tammy and *my* business?"

She held my eyes, and usually, I would have given in.

I was an easygoing guy, for the most part.

My childhood had made my sticking points few and far between—when a kid was just doing his level best to survive, sticking points were really for those who had the luxury to actually have them—*but* when I had one, I didn't cave.

No matter what.

I just made sure to only fight battles that mattered.

Shifting my eyes from hers back to the pan, I flipped the omelet and waited.

Not long, because she knew me, knew the truth about my sticking points. She sighed and muttered, "No, you don't. But Tal—"

"Mags," I warned.

She pushed on, resting her head on my shoulder. "She's a good person. She's been through—" Cutting herself off, she straightened, carried the grater to the sink. "Just . . . please, treat her with kindness. She deserves that and so much more."

My heart pounded in my chest, the need to delve deeper, to find out what she'd been through great.

But it wasn't Mags' story to tell.

It was Tammy's.

So, I just turned back to the pan, removed the first omelet, and asked, "You think she'll want the works, too?"

CHAPTER FOURTEEN

Tammy

I HADN'T MEANT to eavesdrop.

But once I'd started, once I'd heard Maggie say *She's fine. You're fine. We'll sort this out,* I hadn't been able to stop.

At first, I'd thought the *sorting out* was getting me to leave.

But then I'd heard Tal curse the paparazzi and had remembered the flashes from the night before and quickly realized that the sorting out wasn't about them trying to get me to do an extra-long walk of shame. Rather, it was about how to navigate the troves of photographers apparently clustered outside.

As I was processing that—wondering what the photographs looked like, wondering how bad it was if they, as people in the industry, were concerned, wondering what my brother would think, what the guys at the department would say at me having saved some big shot—Mags and Talbots' conversation had grown lighter . . . and I'd been struck mute.

On one hand, I was a little jealous of their obvious closeness. On the other, I was exceptionally touched by the way Talbot had refused to explain himself or our . . . *interlude*—and I was sticking with calling it an *interlude*—to Maggie.

He'd said it was something that was between *us*.

That sounded nice.

To be an *us*.

I hadn't really ever been part of an *us*, not even in my marriage. So, at least, I hadn't been in an *us* since I was six years old, and my mom had died. My dad had stepped up, raising my brother and me by himself, but there still hadn't been an *us*, still hadn't been that connection, that closeness. And I'd missed it terribly—the cooking together in the kitchen, the cuddles in bed, the walking me to school. As an adult, I could understand that my dad had been reeling, had just been trying to survive the loss of his wife, his sudden role becoming the primary care-giver. He'd needed to become the one to remember school lunches and special events, who'd been responsible for birthday parties and taking me to buy new clothes. But he'd been in over his head, and as a consequence, my brother and I had fended for ourselves a lot.

And we'd missed out on a lot. No big parties, no special lunches, no cute clothes. He hadn't remembered to buy tickets to the school carnival, and he certainly hadn't left me hand-written notes in my lunchbox.

Different.

It had all become so different.

I'd taken on a lot, certainly too much, but also not enough, because we'd drifted apart, those ties my mom had built, the ones keeping us together, stretching taut, some severing altogether.

Eventually, it had been my dad, my brother, and I, all existing in three separate spheres. Different planets orbiting the sun, none ever getting close enough to interact.

And I'd missed it. Missed my mom, missed my family.

I'm sure that's why I started looking for that connection in others, why several of my list of twenty men weren't just because I'd been looking for a fun time. I'd used them to search for something deeper . . . and I hadn't found it.

Not even during my short-lived marriage. It had been him and a me, Steven and Tammy, two separate bubbles of living, and those domains had never fully meshed.

I was searching and searching and never finding.

Then I just hadn't been able to take it anymore.

I'd rather be on my own than coming home every day, looking into the eyes of a man who said he loved me, but if he did, it wasn't in the right way. He didn't light up when he saw me, didn't know when I was hurting or sad inside, when I needed to be coddled or pushed. Perhaps, it was me freezing him out, me so used to being that isolated sphere, but Steven also hadn't loved me enough to push his way in.

He, just like my dad, had been happy to let the status quo slide.

And every day, I'd felt increasingly smothered by the warring of expectations and hopes and reality, their fingers wrapping around my neck and slowly, inexorably tightening.

Until . . . I hadn't been able to breathe.

Goodbye Denver, hello Chicago. Then Salt Lake. Then . . . right back in Darlington, still searching for something, and still not finding it.

Sighing, I straightened my shoulders, prepared myself to enter the kitchen.

Then Maggie spoke again. "She's a good person. She's been through—" A pause. "Just . . . please, treat her with kindness. She deserves that and so much more."

My heart squeezed, and I couldn't decide if I should be filled with happiness that she obviously cared deeply or mortification that she thought she needed to counsel someone to treat me nicely. That she thought I needed pity kindness.

Either. Both. All three.

I wanted to run, but I'd been standing in the hall, frozen, listening to them to talk for going on five minutes. I needed to go in and face the gauntlet. Later I could untangle the rest of what was happening in my brain.

"You think she'll want the works, too?" I heard Talbot ask.

And I knew I just needed to get this over with. Forcing my feet to move, to carry me into the kitchen, I said, "The works sounds great."

Two pairs of eyes turned in my direction, two gazes settled on me—wary and hopeful, Talbot's; curious and tentative, Maggie's.

"Morning," I said cheerfully.

Talbot poured eggs into a pan, topped it with some colorful ingredients and cheese, then crossed over to me, those gold eyes holding mine. He brushed the backs of his knuckles lightly down my throat, making my skin pebble with goose bumps, my pulse increase to a rapid tattoo in my veins. "You okay?"

Unable to speak, as was far too often the case with this man, I just nodded.

"Your arm?"

"Fine," I managed.

"I'll rebandage it after omelets."

My lips parted, a protest on the edge of them—something along the lines of *I can take care of that*—but he'd already turned back to the stove, where he executed some crazy wrist-flick, pan-jerk thing and effortlessly flipped the omelet on the pan, before crossing the kitchen, picking up a plate and handing it to Maggie. "Eat," he ordered. "Before it gets cold."

Maggie—who I'd purposefully been avoiding looking at until that moment, for obvious reasons—was raptly watching us, her eyes going from me to Talbot and back again.

But, to her credit, she didn't comment, just picked up her fork.

Or, I should say she didn't comment on the whole finding-us-naked thing. Instead, she looked at me. "I heard you were hurt," she said gently. "You okay?"

I nodded. "Just wasn't fast enough to avoid the knife. It's not a bad . . . what?"

She shook herself, crossing over to me, taking my hand, and

bringing me over to the stools. "You're talking about getting stabbed by a knife like it's not a big deal."

"I barely even felt it," I said, giving in to her shepherding me onto the stool and just sitting down. "I'm not trying to say it *didn't* hurt, especially afterward. But adrenaline is a wonderful and powerful drug."

"But not illicit," Talbot murmured in my ear, making me jump. He kissed the lobe before I could react further and set a plate in front of me, and then Maggie's again forgotten plate in front of her. "She's a tough chick," he told my friend. "I hadn't even processed what was happening when she'd already reacted, ordering the man to the ground." He leaned on the counter, hip next to my elbow. I could feel the heat of him, wanted to drift closer so I could lean against him.

"It doesn't bother you that she saved the day, and you were just standing there?"

"No," he said. "Would I have loved to have superhero skills like her, being able to take out a bad guy with ease? Sure. But was I also so damned thankful she was there? Yes."

"I'm right here," I muttered, reaching for the fork that was laid out on the plate and scooping a huge bite into my mouth.

"I know," Talbot said, tugging lightly at a strand of my damp hair.

Which, by the way, felt like absolute silk after those miracle products.

"I hate that she got hurt," he continued, not releasing the strand, making me shiver as he rolled it between thumb and forefinger. "That's what I'm upset about. Not that she had the skill to protect herself, and luckily for my sorry ass, me as well."

"Well—" Maggie began.

"Did they find out who the perpetrator was?" was my desperate attempt to get the conversational topic off me.

I couldn't lie and say it didn't feel good, the nice things they were saying.

It was just . . . too much.

Plus, the painkillers were starting to wear off.

Silence.

Then Maggie nodded. "Not yet," she whispered. "It's still touch and go. He survived the surgery, but when the police searched his belongings and the immediate area, they didn't find any identification." A beat. "I don't think it'll be long, though. The pictures are everywhere. Someone will ID him soon enough."

I froze with the fork an inch from my mouth. "Define *everywhere*."

Talbot nudged my plate closer. "Eat your omelet first."

I glanced up at him. "And where's yours?"

A smile, a nod toward the stove. "There."

"And don't you have to do your fancy wrist-flick thing to turn it?"

"Probably," he said. But didn't move.

Sighing, I scooped up my abandoned bite, shoved it into my mouth, and only then did he release my hair, push away from the counter, and head back to the cooktop. He did the wrist-flick, and I watched him as he put the omelet on his own plate.

"Are you okay?" Maggie asked quietly. "Like really, actually, okay?"

I tore my gaze from his back, from the hard lines I'd had my hands all over not long before. I faced my friend. "I'm really okay," I whispered. "I promise."

She patted my forearm. "This is going to be rough," she said, voice still quiet, gentleness having invaded, as well. "They are going to be relentless, going to be desperate to find out every last thing about you and your family." A beat. "If you haven't called Mark, you should."

"My brother doesn't want to hear from me," I said. "I can promise you that much."

Another pat, sympathetic this time. "I still think you should call him. You can give him my contact information, just so he has a lifeline in case anything gets really bad on his front."

She was being logical.

I didn't want that logic. I'd been burned by my brother more than a few times over the last years, striving for a connection, even moving to Salt Lake to be closer to him and his family. I'd switched departments, leaving the PD in Chicago for just that reason—well, for that reason and also the windchill—but I'd only been in town for three months before he'd up and moved his family to Seattle.

Leaving me to fend for myself.

Again.

Sigh.

"I'll call him," I said. "Except—"

"What?"

"My purse and suitcase were in the car, both of which I'm assuming are evidence now."

Talbot dragged a stool closer, sitting right next to me, making it very difficult for me to focus on anything except for the fact that he was so near, and I wanted to spend more quality time with his body.

Mags' gaze flicked over my shoulder then she rolled her eyes and ate another bite of her food.

"The car is in my garage," he said. "Your purse and suitcase are by the front door."

I glanced down at my body, positively swimming in his T-shirt and sweatpants. "Then why am I wearing your clothes?"

An unrepentant grin. "Because I wanted you to."

My mouth fell open.

Then Maggie chuckled, and I glared at her then twisted to glare at Talbot for good measure. "Neither of you are funny."

Hot breath in my ear. "Good thing I wasn't trying to be."

I shivered, found myself leaning closer. I really shouldn't be. But the man was like freaking catnip. "Good thing . . ." *Gah.* I lost whatever retort I'd had prepared when his front met my back and he snagged my fork, picking up another bite and lifting it to my mouth.

"Eat," he murmured.

"I—"

He slid the tines in between my lips, and I swear to God, if the man wasn't so sexy, if the omelet with all of its works weren't so freaking delicious, I would have snatched that fork back and put it through his right eyeball.

Very specific? Yes.

Very truthful? No.

Also, if I were being realistic, my retort probably wouldn't have been a good one anyway.

He scooped up another bite and plunked it into my mouth when I started to form another protest. Not that my protest would have mattered. I was starting to see that this man was very much a force to be reckoned with. I needed to get my shit together and find a way to hold my own, even with all of his yumminess pressed to all of my . . . none-i-ness?

Fuck, Conners, that was bad.

So bad, in fact, that I found myself snorting at my inner monologue, drawing the focus of both Maggie and Talbot. Maggie, I could see, her brown eyes sparkling with interest as they studied me—or rather me and Talbot pressed to my back. Talbot, on the other hand, I couldn't see, not with him still at my back, but I knew he was looking at me, just knew it.

How? Someone might ask.

Idiocy and instinct, I might reply.

Another snort escaped me, more focus settling my way, but I didn't acknowledge either of them, just plunked the fork out of Tal's hand, started eating in earnest, and then used the remainder of my available brainpower to wonder how in the hell I'd gotten here.

Unfortunately, I didn't have any answer, other than to blame the gun . . . oh, and the knife, too.

CHAPTER FIFTEEN

Talbot

I DON'T THINK Tammy realized how bad it was until after we finished eating and Maggie sat us down in the family room and pulled out her laptop.

She brought up screen after screen, too many articles to ever read, blog posts galore, photos and YouTube videos, Instagram stories and tweets. There was even an entire thread on TikTok that had gone viral. The attack had been covered in everything from gossip sheets to all those social media influencers to local news to national papers. It was, in a word, everywhere.

Tammy grew quieter with each page that came up, with the news clips and the comments that followed.

The only good thing was that the paparazzi had caught everything.

The older man, his face lined and drawn, his eyes huge and sunken. I had to admit he looked frighteningly crazed on the videos, much more so than I'd been able to comprehend the night before with everything moving so fast. They showed the man lunging toward us, the knife held above his head.

They'd caught Tammy's warning to stop.

They'd caught the first shot and then him getting back up again, where they'd also filmed the rest of it. Tammy firing twice more, kicking the knife away, and then immediately trying to save the man.

All with blood pouring down her arm because he'd cut her with that knife, and in that sexy black dress.

She was fucking amazing.

She was a fucking superhero.

And right now, people seemed to realize it.

But sooner or later, that tide would turn, someone would find something to exploit or frown upon or to rally the forces against her. I needed to make sure that didn't happen.

I needed *Maggie* to make sure that didn't happen.

"Right now," my publicist was saying, "they haven't identified you, yet. That's a good thing. That gives us time to figure out how we want to play this. You'll want to release a statement soon, though, otherwise the frenzy will continue. We can consult with your lawyer"—Maggie's gaze came to mine, and I nodded, assuring her that Tammy would have access to any of my resources I could supply her with—"and figure out what we can say—"

"No."

I blinked, glanced at Tammy, whose skin had gone ashen.

"No, I don't want a statement," she whispered. "I want to forget that ever happened. I want to just go back to my life and—" Her voice broke as she closed the laptop. "This isn't right. I-I *hurt* someone. He might die, and those people out there"—she threw an arm out in the direction of the front gate—"they don't even care. They're feeding on it, consuming it like it's some funny meme or a hair dyeing video. And a man is fighting for his life in the hospital because *I* shot him." A beat, her angry stare almost a physical lash as it landed on me. "And you're part of it. Both of you."

Words escaped me.

I didn't have words that would take that angst away, that would make what she said any less true.

Because she was right.

But being right didn't negate the fact that we had to do something, and we needed to do it quickly.

I pushed up from the couch, felt the barest blip of hesitation when she shot cold, hazel eyes in my direction, then promptly ignored it. She was upset; she was in pain—if the lines fanning out from the corners of her mouth were any indication—and she was in a new scenario with absolutely no clue how to proceed.

Anyone would be feeling adrift and angry and uncertain.

So, I ignored that blip of wavering and just took her in my arms.

"You're right," I said, finding the words much easier with her close, her head tucked beneath my chin, the strands of her hair, still damp from the shower, brushing along my arm. "Of course, you're right. This whole situation is fucked. People wanted to sell every consumable portion, to push papers and views and ads and merch, but none of that changes the fact that I would have very likely been seriously injured last night, if not for you." I cupped her jaw, tilted her head back. "I might have died, if not for you."

Her lips parted. "I'm sure—"

"Did it seem like any of them were coming to my aid last night?"

"There was that one girl—"

"One," I said. "Yeah, and what good would that have done me? Her standing on the opposite side of the road, camera poised as a man ran at me with a knife." I stroked my thumb back and forth across her cheek. "You saved me, and besides protecting you from this media storm, that's the only thing that matters."

"Why?" she whispered.

"Because no one has ever done that for me before."

Her brows pulled together. "What do you mean?"

"My parents were drug addicts, Pretty Eyes. They were sick and so wrapped up in their addictions that they couldn't think of anything but getting their next fix." I shrugged, not to dismiss it, exactly, since it was my experience, but because . . . that had been *my* experience. I was used to it. I couldn't say that it wasn't completely painless, because, fuck, it did hurt sometimes. But I'd long ago learned that it was over. They had both been gone for a long time. My mom had OD'd right in front of me, my dad had left me to the system and disappeared. For all I knew, he'd succumbed to the drugs just as my mother had.

That kind of trauma left a hole.

That kind of trauma had left me feeling empty for a long, long time.

Then I'd met Maggie, and she'd filled in a little of that crevice, right along with Pierce and Artie, Eden and Damon, all of them continuing to backfill the emptiness. Now, I wasn't quite so hollow.

But now, I was much more aware of what I'd lost, what I was still missing out on.

That longing was real and intense . . . and made me aware of exactly how precious this woman in front of me was.

"I'm sorry," she whispered.

"It is what it is," I told her. "They're gone now, have been gone for a long time." I sucked in a short breath, released it just as rapidly. "But the thing is that I don't remember a time when a person protected me from harm."

Those pretty hazel eyes flashed. "Maggie—"

I nodded. "No," I said. "You're right about that. Maggie is a good person, and she has weathered many a professional storm with me. She's one of my closest friends for sure, but"—and here I admitted the truth that I'd held deep in my heart—"it's not quite the same as what you did, because you're not on my payroll." Guilt creeping in, I glanced over my shoulder to catch

Mags' gaze, to apologize, even though it was a painful fact I'd long held close, but she wasn't in the room.

She'd gone.

And my heart squeezed, knowing that she *was* a good friend, the absolute best, even as the understanding of what I'd admitted still held true.

I loved Maggie.

I just . . . it was hard to separate what she felt for me when I was the one signing her paychecks. Perhaps that wasn't fair. *No,* I knew it wasn't, but it was also what I felt, as unfair as it was.

"I could understand that," Tammy murmured. "But she loves you. She would do anything to make sure you're safe."

I knew that, too.

"It's not the same," I whispered. "You didn't get anything out of helping me. In fact, you're probably only going to get screwed because your personal life is going to be infiltrated, you're going to have to deal with the media following you until this eventually blows over. You helped me, and because of that, you're fucked."

"I'm not fucked." She covered my hand with her own, and I half-expected her to tug it off. But then she simply kept it there. "I help people because it's my job, because I'm trained to do it. It's instinct to step in."

Ouch.

Ouch.

Perhaps that was worse than Maggie being my friend and employee. No, it definitely *was* worse because this was a woman I cared about, far too much for the all of one day I'd known her, had only helped me because it was her job, her calling to save people.

It was not about me.

Probably the nearly physical slap of that thought slamming around my brain, sending my ears ringing, my heart thudding, shouldn't have been a surprise. Maybe it was all about my ego being pricked, me being brought back down to earth like all the rest of the populace.

But all I could think was . . . fuck, that hurt.

I swallowed, gently peeled my hand from her cheek, and retreated a step.

"I'll be right back."

"Tal . . ."

God, why did she have to call me that? Hardly anyone shortened my name, and certainly no one made it sound like she did—gentle, with an edge of need. The longing I felt from my shortened name on her tongue was intense. I wanted her to call me that, to use that tone, forever.

Meanwhile, I was just a responsibility, her contribution to the universe, a police officer doing her job, a decent woman doing a nice thing.

"I . . . um . . ." I glanced toward the hall, wanting, no *needing* to escape. "You know what? I forgot I needed to do . . . something," I said. "I'll be right back."

Turning and heading out of the room, I almost mowed Maggie down in the hallway but managed to catch her arm and steady her before I all but ran for my bedroom like an upset teenager.

Pathetic.

Probably.

But I was feeling as lovestruck and heartbroken as one, so it fit.

CHAPTER SIXTEEN

Tammy

I'D HURT HIM.

I hadn't meant to, but I'd done it anyway.

And now, I felt like the absolute biggest jackass on the planet. I took a step toward the hall, intending on following him, but Maggie caught my wrist.

"It's better to let him have his space when he's like this."

Jealously. *Again.*

That she knew this man better than I did, when I hadn't even known Talbot for more than twenty-four hours. It was ludicrous to feel that way, and yet, I'd been compartmentalizing things left and right, willy-nilly over the last day.

What was one more?

I'd just pretend that I wasn't falling for a very unsuitable man, that our two lives—wholly different and completely incompatible—would go on without the slightest hiccup or speed bump.

Also—side note to my pretending—Maggie had another thing coming if she thought I was going to leave that man hurting until he managed to pull a mask around himself enough to fake being fine. I had too much fucking experience at doing that to willingly allow another person to do it under my watch.

To do it because of *me*.

I shook her off. Gently, because it was Maggie. Then took another step toward the hall.

Her voice trailed me. "Let's talk about what we should—"

"I don't care about shoulds," I said. "I'm going to talk to him."

"It's better—"

I spun back to face her. "With all due respect, I don't give a fuck about *better* right now." And with that, I strode down the hall, glancing in each room of the giant house as I walked, searching for the man in question and not finding him until I opened the closed bedroom door.

He didn't move from his position, staring out the large glass windows, even though I wasn't particularly quiet when I walked in.

And I knew I had a choice.

I could walk back out. I could re-enter my own sphere, stay isolated and safe in the status quo. Keep on pretending for an eternity. Or . . . I could take the universe's signal that this man, this situation was completely dissimilar from anything I'd experienced before and jump in with both feet. I could pop that bubble, risk getting close, because the circumstances might be different.

Because this man might be different.

But *could* I?

Risk my heart, my hope again. Because as much as I talked a big game about pretending, the organ was ready to flop over and expose its vulnerable underbelly to this man.

Alarm bells blared, the urge to turn and flee was real . . . but my feet didn't carry me out of the room.

Instead, I closed the door and walked over to him, stopping a foot from his back as I struggled to find the words. I didn't have anything sweet or romantic to say, didn't have anything but the blunt truth.

So, he'd have to handle the blunt truth.

"Yes, I saved you because it was my job, because I would have done the same thing for anyone who was encountering that situation."

His spine was ramrod straight, the muscles on the backs of his arms standing out in sharp relief when he clenched his hands into fists, and I swore I could hear his teeth grinding.

I kept talking anyway.

"I'm trained to do that," I said. "I'm the type of person who cannot stand to see someone suffering without doing something about it." Here, I faltered because he whipped around, his eyes absolutely blazing as they locked onto mine. "But—" I cleared my throat as he stepped closer, my heart thudding, my lips tingling. "But I wasn't afraid for myself last night," I whispered. "I was terrified for you, terrified that something would happen to you. Not because of the cameras—I didn't even notice them until after it was all over. But because I was scared that *you* would get hurt."

By the time I finished pushing that out, my lips were parted, breaths coming in rapid gusts, my pulse thundering in my veins.

He didn't say anything for a long moment.

Then his throat worked, and he rasped out, "Tammy."

And I did the only thing I could think of. I closed the distance between us, wrapped my arms around his waist, and hugged him tight. "I didn't—I couldn't have you think that my actions were strictly about you, because that would be a lie. I am who I am. I help people because I can." I squeezed tighter, a relieved breath sliding out from between my lips when his arms wrapped around me in turn. "But I'm glad I was there to help you. I'm glad that I could save you, that you didn't get hurt because . . ."

"Why, baby?" he whispered hoarsely.

The words tumbled out.

"Because I don't think I want to live in a world where you're not in it."

It should have been a ridiculous, overly emotional statement. But I meant it, as scary as that thought was.

His arms convulsed, and I buried my face in his chest, feeling incredibly vulnerable and worried that I might be revisiting stupid with a capital S, but also knowing that I'd spoken the truth.

For better or worse, it *was* the truth.

Acceptance slid through me as I stood there with my body against Talbot's, his fingers in my hair, his arms around me, his warm heat surrounding me.

"Thank you," he whispered, what seemed like an eternity later, his hold loosening, his embrace loosening. His palm came to my jaw again, cupping it in a hand roughened with callouses.

God, I loved it—his touch, that hand—so much that I found my filter completely gone, my next words exploding on an all too easy blurt.

"Your hand isn't smooth."

His face registered surprise before his golden eyes were molten. "Swordplay."

My brows rose. Um. "What?"

"My next film is set in King Arthur's times," he said. "I'm a knight."

Somehow that was absolutely fitting. "Is the armor shining?" I asked lightly, my lips tipping up. "Or dinged and rusty?"

A chuckle that caressed my skin like a thousand intangible fingers. "Hopefully, the first." A shrug. "But probably, the second." He shrugged again. "Let's just say that I'm a knight with some baggage."

I grinned. "I can't wait to see it."

His hand twitched on my cheek, an emotion I couldn't decipher trailing across his face before it was replaced with something I could. With amusement. "The swordplay?" he asked innocently.

A snort. "That, too."

He waggled his brows. "But"—more mock innocence here —"I thought I already did."

I stepped out of his arms, rolled my eyes. "Well, clearly you're feeling better, so I'm just going to go."

I turned for the door.

An arm slipped around my waist, reeled me back in.

"Tammy?" he asked, his lips very close to my ear.

"Hmm?"

He spun me, stared deep into my eyes.

"I'm going to kiss you now."

My lips curved, and I rose on tiptoe.

Then I kissed him first.

CHAPTER SEVENTEEN

Talbot

BY THE TIME I managed to stop kissing Tammy and extricate us from the bedroom, Maggie had arranged a command center in the family room.

Two laptops open.

Her cell phone on the table.

Piles of paper stacked on every available inch.

She glanced up when we walked in, and her smile didn't hide her concern. I saw it in her eyes, pressed into the lines around her face. But her voice was natural when she patted the couch next to her and said, "Let's take a look at what I've put together."

I nodded, and still holding Tammy's hand, I sat on the couch. Which meant that she was stuck sitting beside me.

Muhaha.

Not that she was looking at me. Not in the least. She was staring at the screen on the laptop, and I turned my gaze there.

"Oh, my God," she whispered.

"What?" I asked. She'd already seen a lot of this earlier.

"That's *The New York Times*," she sputtered. "I—oh, my God.

This is just—" She popped to her feet. "How can I be in it? And on CNN? And—" Her hands came up to her hair, gripping tightly before she winced and dropped the hurt one back to her side.

I snagged her hand. "It's a slow news cycle right now. It'll blow over." Said with much more confidence than I actually felt. "Maggie's got a plan, and—" I turned to look at my publicist. "You have a plan, right?"

Maggie nodded. "Right. I do have a plan. I promise, we'll take care of this," she said, standing and placing her hand on Tammy's shoulder. "It'll be okay."

Tammy, her face pale, nodded and sat back down on the couch. "Okay," she murmured, swallowing hard. "I had a minor freak-out there, but I'm fine. Really, I'm fine." Her eyes went to Maggie's. "What do I have to do to get back to my life?"

Mags' gaze came to mine, just for a brief moment, but I saw the question on its surface, the concern in its depths.

I didn't want Tammy to go back to her life.

I wanted her to become part of mine.

But that wasn't fair, and now it was my turn to protect her.

I nodded. "Tell me what I have to do."

Fingers weaving with mine, a warm shoulder pressed to my side. "No," Tammy said, surprising the hell out of me. "Tell us what *we* have to do."

Mags was quiet for just a brief moment, her gaze still filled with questions, that concern still there, but she nodded, smiled, and moved back to the couch, sitting down and picking up the first of many papers. "Okay," she said. "Here's the first step."

———

"THANKS, MAGS," I whispered, giving her a hug before she slipped out my front door.

"Oh, hey." She stopped, glanced back, and I didn't miss the flash of the cameras from beyond the gate. She noticed, too, coming closer, deliberately angling her body to block any good shots of me.

"What's up?"

"Be good to her, okay?"

"Mags," I began, thinking she was going to tell me not to hurt her friend, to treat her with kindness and respect.

I didn't need another version of that talk from her.

I'd give it to Tammy regardless of Maggie's interference.

She squeezed my wrist. "I wasn't finished," she murmured. "Be good to yourself, too, okay? You deserve to be someone's whole world, to have them light up for you, to be the thing that makes their life better."

A shaking exhale. "Mags," I said again.

She patted my chest. "I'll release the statement tonight, and we'll give it a couple of days before we go to our next step."

"Okay."

"Enjoy being secluded." She hugged me, her lips going to my ear and whispering, "And enjoy Tammy." I smiled, joy bubbling inside me like it was a living thing, a babbling brook, washing over me in wonderful, cool dribbles. Then with a pat on my arm, she turned and walked toward her car.

I watched her back it up, maneuver toward the gate, pausing to gesture to me through the driver's side window to go back inside.

Smiling, I did so.

But I still kept an eye on her through the blinds, making sure she made it through okay. I hadn't needed to worry, however, as members of the security team magically appeared, pushing back the crowd and helping Maggie navigate her car out. I kept watching until they were back inside the gate, until that metal panel was closed, and then I double-checked the front door was locked and the blinds were drawn before heading toward the back of the house where Tammy and I were doing our secluding.

I wished I'd moved already.

I hated that there was a line of sight from the gate to the front of the house, had hated it since the moment I'd bought this place.

This wasn't the first time that I'd had paparazzi outside.

It was just the first time they'd stayed after getting a couple of shots.

"Tal?"

I glanced up, realized I'd stopped in the middle of the hall.

Tammy had swapped my sweats for a pair of black leggings, but I was unreasonably thrilled that she'd decided to keep wearing my T-shirt.

"What's up, Hazel Eyes?"

Her mouth twitched. "I'm hungry. Is it okay if I make us something to eat?"

Us. Not herself.

My heart thudded, and if it weren't such a cliché response, I'd say that my stomach was filled with butterflies. How else to describe that fluttering, swirling feeling?

Fingers on my jaw. "You okay?"

I covered her hand. "Anything in this house—including me —is at your disposal. You don't have to ask before you use something or raid the pantry for snacks."

"You say that now," she murmured. "But this is before I start raiding your underwear drawer."

My head jerked. "Um, why would you raid my underwear drawer?"

A shrug, her hand sliding away. "Because boxer briefs are the most comfortable things to sleep in ever."

I lifted a brow, even though she couldn't see it, as she'd already turned for the kitchen. "How do you know I wear boxer briefs?"

She paused, glanced back at me over her shoulder. "Don't you?"

That was beside the point.

A smile. "I'm right." She spun back and disappeared

inside the kitchen. I followed her, saw that she'd gone straight for the fridge. My eyes flicked to the window beyond the sink —it was the only one that faced the front of the property— made sure the blinds I'd closed the night before were still shut.

The French doors facing toward the patio were open, and since the sun had begun to set, the early evening sky was darkening, swathes of deep purple and rust and cobalt drifting across the horizon.

Beautiful.

But it still didn't hold a candle to the woman who'd just pulled out a stack of food from the fridge and was organizing it just so on the counter.

"How many people are you feeding over there?"

"One," she said, grinning mischievously over at me.

"What happened to *us?*"

"Two," she amended. "If the other part of our duo can rustle up a couple of beers?"

I moved around the island, standing very close to her back, inhaling until the floral spice of her filled my nose, settled like a second membrane around my cells. "And what if I can't?"

A smile over her shoulder. "I'm open to bribes."

"How very mercenary of you."

"You know what they say about the police," she quipped, finishing lining up the ingredients and bending to open the drawer beneath the cooktop. Since I didn't back up, I had the great benefit of feeling her ass brush against me.

No, not *me.*

Against my cock, which instantly hardened. Once had definitely not been enough.

Her eyes met mine over her shoulder.

Short of seeing her naked, it might have been the sexiest thing I'd ever seen, those hazel eyes hooded, the pupils dilated. "You have chef fantasies?"

"I have *you* fantasies." My hands dropped to her hips. "And

I don't know what they say about other officers, but I'm just kidding. You're the furthest thing from mercenary there is."

A flicker across her eyes, and she straightened.

"What?"

"Do you like chicken?" she asked, setting the pan on the burner. Then she laughed. "Of course, you like it. It was in your fridge." She side-stepped, causing my hands to drop, as she began opening and closing cabinets. "Where do you keep cutting boards in this joint?"

"Tammy."

"Ah," she said, opening one more and then pulling out a plastic surface to cut on. "There they are. This is just what I needed." Another smile over her shoulder, though this one was so fake that it almost hurt to look at. "You ready for my world-famous, or well, my inside-my-own-house famous chicken parmesan? It's delicious."

I stepped closer, dropped one hand on either side of her, trapping her between my body and the counter. "I'm sure it is," I murmured. "But I'm more worried about what put that look on your face."

Her spine was perfectly straight, a rigid line that gave steel poles a run for their money. "I don't know what you're talking about." She set down the cutting board. "I hope you're hungry," she blathered, words a mile a minute, "because maybe I'll make cookies after this. It's been ages, and I took another pain pill and look!" Tammy lifted her arm over her head. "I can do this. Isn't that amazing?"

"Amazing," I agreed, snagging her wrist and drawing her arm back down, lest she accidentally hurt herself in her avoidance. "Tam—"

She crumpled, that spine curving, a pole bent over after a collision with a car, that strong material damaged and warped, and I knew that I couldn't push this. If she wanted to be cheerful and cook and pretend nothing had just flitted across her face, I'd let her—

Fuck, that sounded egotistical.

But my point was I didn't have any hold over her, she wasn't beholden to my whims, didn't owe me an explanation.

In truth, I had all the owing locked down firmly in my corner

"I love chicken parmesan," I said, stroking my fingers down the back of her neck. "What can I do to help?"

That spine straightening, her body slowly shifting around to face me, and this time, the flash I could decipher in her eyes wasn't old pain, wasn't something dark and barbed. Instead, it was . . . gentle.

She brushed her fingers over my jaw, and every single time she did that, every time she initiated contact, my heart skipped a beat. Her lips parted, a breath sliding out, coating my skin, and then she murmured, "Those beers would be really nice."

"How about a soda since you're on drugs?"

She made a face, but then she smiled at me, warmth shining out of her eyes like the sun bright overhead on a summer's night.

Heart thumping against my ribs—the woman was *full* of powerful magic—I stepped back, went to the fridge hidden in the island, the one where all my wine and beer was stored, pulled out two cans of soda, and popped the tops. I plunked one next to her then hoisted myself up on the counter, watching as Tammy scavenged through my cabinets, muttering to herself the whole time.

With lithe curves and about six inches shorter than me, she was temptation personified, and I found myself watching her lips move as she spoke quietly to herself, the line of her throat exposed and calling for my kiss. I'd checked on her stitches earlier, and they were carefully wrapped in another bandage, but I believed her about the wound not hurting, or at least not very much. Even without the pain pills, she was a tough chick, not complaining at all during the day as we'd planned things out with Maggie, but as the hours had passed, I'd seen the signs, was glad that Mags had, too.

Our friend had pleaded traffic and needing to get home to her fiancé, but I hadn't missed the fact that she'd located Tammy's prescription and placed the bottle on the table before she'd left.

Luckily, the gesture had worked.

Tammy had taken the pills, and now I didn't have to worry about shoving one down her throat. That pleasant image—not —aside, I was glad she wasn't hurting and was going to leave it at that.

"Tammy?" I asked, swinging my feet back and forth.

"What's up?" she said, sprinkling herbs onto the chicken.

"Where you'd learn to cook?"

Her eyes came to mine. "How do you mean?" she asked, slicing into some tomatoes and then dropping them into a pot of boiling water.

"I mean," I said, reaching for a piece of carrot as she moved onto a fresh cutting board, prepping ingredients for a salad. "How did you learn to cook? My skills come from culinary boot camp before a movie." I smiled when she glanced up at me, surprise on her face. "I'm guessing yours didn't come via the same."

"Not so much," she said, chopping a cucumber. "Mine came via necessity."

I lifted my brows.

She glanced down at the board, was quiet for so long that I expected her to not answer. Then, surprisingly, she did. "My dad raised my brother and me for most of our lives." Her face did that thing, the twisting, barbs hidden beneath the surface thing. I'd seen it twice now, and I already decided that it was the most awful thing I'd ever seen.

"So, it was a matter of survival then?"

Her lips twitched. "In a manner of speaking," she said. "What did you eat before you went to chef school?"

"Ramen noodles," I said, telling her the truth.

"And?" she asked, waving a hand.

"And ramen noodles."

"That's it?"

I shrugged. "I was a starving actor. They were cheap and came in bulk. It was the perfect food."

"Except for your arteries," she said. "The salt in them alone will kill you. How did you keep your body"—a wave of that knife, down and up in the direction of my torso—"in that kind of shape?"

I waggled my brows. "What kind of shape are you referring to?"

She snorted, went back to chopping the cucumber. "You know exactly the shape."

"You should also know that this is my job," I said. "I hate exercising, but only do it for one, roles, and for two, so I don't get so giant and out of shape that I bite it prematurely."

"All of this"—another wave of the knife—"is normal?"

"I told you, I have a movie role coming up," I said, giving in to the urge to run my fingers through her hair. It was like silk, even though she'd done absolutely nothing to it except to allow it to hang over her shoulders and air dry.

"So swordplay is responsible for all that . . . yumminess?" Heat in her eyes.

I smiled at being referred to as *yumminess*. "No," I said. "This—" I couldn't resist lifting my shirt, just a little bit. Because while I might hate exercising, I didn't hate the way Tammy looked at the product of said exercise.

She made a garbled noise, dropped her gaze to the cutting board. "This what?"

I shifted a little closer. "This is leftover from my last project . . ." I named the superhero film that I'd just wrapped, pleasure sliding through me when her eyes widened.

"Are you really going to be in that?" she breathed.

More pleasure at her being so excited. Maybe I could get her a set visit if we had to do any reshoots. I'd bet she'd get a kick out of meeting my female co-star, who was headlining the film. Bri was seriously awesome.

"I am."

"Wow." Her knife continued clicking on the cutting board. "Color me suitably impressed."

"Yeah?"

The edge of her smile was just barely visible, a tiny upside-down rainbow creasing her cheek. "Yeah."

Quiet descended, and I watched her chop and cut and prep like a pro. Sure, there weren't any flourishes or fancy flips of the pan, but there was a quiet efficiency about her movements that I admired. Graceful and clean, without anything extra added in.

Which was more than could be said of my own chef skills.

I was all flourish, all flash.

"Ramen noodles," she said again, that tipsy-topsy rainbow making another appearance as she shook her head.

"Truthfully, they're a godsend." I chuckled. "Plus, when your water gets turned off, you can even eat them dry."

A shudder. "That sounds horrible."

"I'll turn you on to my delicacy when it's my turn to cook dinner."

"That's not happening."

"Me cooking dinner? Or you trying dry ramen?"

"Both," she said, drizzling some oil into the pan. I focused back on the space in front of her, amazed that she'd somehow filled a bowl with a salad and also coated two chicken breasts with eggs and breadcrumbs. She put them into the pan, where they started sizzling, then went to the sink and washed her hands.

Then she leaned back against the countertop opposite me, and we listened to the food cooking while staring at each other.

Probably it should have been boring.

Instead, it was the most interesting silence of my life.

The way the light played over her skin, the lights above

gilding it. How it passed through her eyes, showcasing all the changing browns and golds and greens in her irises, each glimpse a new and more beautiful combination. She had freckles on her nose, and her top lip was slightly larger than the bottom.

"Tell me about your favorite movie," she said, pushing off the counter and moving back to the pan to flip the chicken.

"You sure you want to hear me blabber on about work?"

"It's got to be more interesting than my job."

"I highly doubt that," I admitted. "It's just a lot of me reading lines and then posing in front of the camera with varying degrees of makeup on."

"Except you get to travel all over the world and pretend to be a different person."

"That is one bonus," I agreed. "Though the travel isn't all it's cracked up to be."

"What do you mean?"

"Well, for example, I just spent the last three months in the desert, scorching during the day, freezing my ass off at night. Filming is always fun because it's the cap on all the hard prep work. But it's just like any job. There are good and bad things."

"I could see that."

"What's something bad about yours?"

"Besides the whole saving someone and then having paparazzi trying to find out my every movement part?"

I smiled as she got to work on peeling the tomatoes, on whipping together a sauce, which she ladled over the chicken. "Yes, *that*."

Her laughter filled the room as she topped everything with cheese then stuck the pan in the oven.

"Is this about the Milk Caper?"

"You remember that?" she asked, closing the door and spinning to face me.

I remembered everything about her, but I couldn't say that. Instead, I just shifted closer and rested my hand on her hip.

"You never did tell me," I said. "It's like I've been on a cliff-hanger for a full day. That's pure torture."

"Clearly, you never read any good books," she said, picking up the bowl of salad and carrying it to the square table that was located in one corner of the kitchen.

I reached into the cabinet behind me, pulled out a couple of plates, collected two more sodas from the fridge, silverware from the drawers, and napkins from the container on the island. Together we set the table, and it was natural, as though it were something we'd done a hundred, a thousand times before.

"What do you mean?" I asked when she didn't elaborate on her statement.

"Good books often end on cliffies. Cliff-hangers," she added when I looked at her, the confusion I felt in my head probably obvious on my face. "Since you think they're torture, then clearly you have no appreciation for the great, gloriousness of an excellent cliff-hanger in the world of literary fiction."

I captured a lock of her hair between thumb and forefinger. "What's your favorite book?"

Her brows lifted, suspicion in her tone. "Why do you ask?"

"Because, apparently I need to expand my horizons."

"And you'll do that by reading my suggestions?"

"Sure, why not?"

More flickers across her face, more barbed memories and pain in those eyes. Then she turned away, the strand of her hair slipping from my fingers, and headed to the oven, peeking inside.

Her voice was quiet as she retrieved a spatula and brought the pan to the table, serving up the breasts, "I really like . . ."

And then she told me about her favorite books, which I jotted down in the notes section of my phone, making mental reminders to buy out Amazon of her suggestions and to get reading.

Her cheeks flushed pink after she'd spoken for several minutes on end, her eyes going to my plate. "Oh God, I've been blabbering on, and you haven't even eaten. Go on," she said, nudging my food closer. "Eat while it's hot, baby. I can't have my world-famous chicken parmesan going to waste."

Baby.

More heart thumping.

But I didn't comment on the endearment, just picked up my fork and knife and began chowing down.

It was delicious.

But I didn't get much chance to eat—or at least not while it was hot—because then she asked me more about my work, and I asked her more about hers. I found out about the adorable little Milk Caper. She found out about my favorite film to date—a small indie one where my character had barely had two lines.

And . . . we just talked.

For hours, eating occasional bits of lukewarm chicken, finishing off the salad, before I got up and retrieved a pint of ice cream from the freezer, sitting next to her at the table instead of across like we'd been positioned over dinner.

"You only grabbed one spoon," she murmured.

I waggled my brows. "I know."

So, over bites of ice cream with a shared spoon, our legs tangling, our bodies leaning closer and closer, we talked about everything and nothing—TV and books, movies we both loved, places to travel that were on our bucket lists. It was one of those conversations that a person never wanted to end.

But then she began yawning, her eyes drooping closed.

I pushed away the empty ice cream container then stood, scooping her into my arms.

"Tal," she murmured.

"What's up, sweetheart?"

"The dishes. I should—" Her head flopped onto my shoulder, another yawn wracking her frame.

My lips curved. "I've got them."

"Doesn't exist."

"Hmm?"

"A man who does dishes . . ." She trailed off. ". . . doesn't . . . ex . . ."

And with that, she fell asleep in my arms. I carried her down the hall, tucked her under the blankets, and returned to do the dishes. Then when I was done, I crammed myself back into that chair at the bedside and slipped into oblivion, studying the peaceful expression on her face.

It was the best night of my life.

Hands down.

CHAPTER EIGHTEEN

Tammy

I woke up with sunlight blinding me through my closed eyes for the second time in as many days.

The man needed to invest in blackout shades.

With my ever-changing shifts at the sheriff's office, they'd become an absolute lifesaver. I could sleep in, never worrying about the position of the sun in the sky, or the giant, gas bastard's rays streaming into my eyelids.

Especially this California sunshine.

It never seemed to quit.

I stretched, my arm aching, but in a way that was much more manageable than the previous day. No heavy-duty painkillers would be needed today, that was for sure, but I might hit up Talbot for some ibuprofen.

Squinting against the sun, I slowly pushed up . . .

And saw Talbot, himself, sleeping in the chair next to the bed, his neck at an angle that had to be uncomfortable, his lips parted slightly, his breathing slow and steady. He hadn't shaved since before the party, and his jaw was filled with stubble, a rough patch I'd felt beneath my fingertips several times the previous day. Now it was even longer, approaching more beard than not, and the man could definitely pull off a beard.

Something buzzed, and my gaze was drawn to the night-stand, where I was surprised to see my cell was plugged in.

Quietly picking it up and trying desperately to not think how far down the rabbit hole of Talbot I'd gone the previous day—straight past keeping distance and right into both feet in the fire—I unplugged my cell and looked at the screen.

Yesterday might have been stupid, but I couldn't bring myself to regret it, not when the man was . . . well, a man I'd always dreamed of.

He'd been thoughtful and kind and . . . I was going to soak that up.

I was too addicted to the way he made me feel to do anything besides that. Who knew the next time I'd be shacked up with a movie star? I might as well live it up.

Now, however, my cell buzzed again.

I glanced down to see the sheriff himself had texted me.

"Fuck," I breathed.

Rob was the one who'd hired me, and as a former detective and newly elected sheriff, I didn't want to piss him off. Not only was he my boss, but he was also my mentor, and he'd taken me under his wing when I'd expressed interest in going for detective.

Not that there was any space on the payroll or in the department for hiring another full-time position, but Rob had still helped me with training and given me opportunities to learn.

He was another one of the good guys.

Too bad he was married.

Trepidation in my veins, my fingertips trembling, I unlocked my screen and read the message.

Report in.

Well, that didn't give much for me to go on, did it?

I had no idea if he was pissed about my newfound media fame—and based on the news stories Mags had shown me the previous day, I would be delusional to think he hadn't heard what happened—or if he was worried for my safety.

I hoped for the second one.

But . . . I worried it might be the first.

Usually, police departments preferred their officers to keep low social profiles.

And being everywhere online, in major newspapers, and on TV didn't bode well for my future as a sheriff's officer.

Kind of hard to prevent crime with a gaggle of cameramen at my back.

Or maybe . . . maybe it was the *best* way.

No one would dare step a toe out of line if it were going to get caught on camera, right? Snorting to myself, I slid quietly from the bed and padded my way across the bedroom, almost desperate for another shower, for another chance to use those yummy-smelling products . . . provide myself with another escape from this conversation.

But I wasn't a coward.

Which was why I slipped through the French door leading out onto that small patio beyond the glass in the bedroom, full of lush greenery. A breeze hit my skin the moment I did, lazy swirls of air catching my hair, drifting along my nape, circling over my arms and legs. Clouds drifted across the sky, tiny puffs of cotton floating along the horizon, transforming from turtle to rabbit to alligator to no end of animal shapes. I spent a moment there, more delaying, but also soaking in this moment, in enjoying that it was quiet, and I was alive.

Then as elephant turned to dolphin, I dialed Rob's number.

"Tammy?" he answered on the second ring, his voice filled with concern. "Are you all right?"

"I'm fine," I said quickly. "Look, about the stories. I'm sorry if this brings attention to the department. I wasn't trying to do that. I just . . . I was there, and it happened, and I—"

"What exactly are you apologizing for?" he asked, his words partly obscured by loud talking in the background.

I heard him walking, the noise quieting as I sputtered, "I —um—I—"

"Let me help you out," he said. "You don't have anything to apologize for. I wanted to make sure you were good, find out if you needed anything."

"Oh, I'm—"

"Don't say fine," he interrupted. "Because you sure as shit can't be fine. Not with your face plastered everywhere." A beat. "I saw the video."

My breath caught.

"You did good, captain."

That breath slid out. "Thanks." And strangely enough, I was close to tears, the backs of my eyes burning, my lungs feeling tight. "I really am fine," I said when I could speak again. "I'm holed up with Talbot until the press calms down, and then I'll be right back at work." I thought about the number of cameras out front. "I might need to take a couple more vacation days before I can come back to my shifts."

"Right. The whole face-plastered-all-over-the-place thing."

I winced. "Yeah."

"You sure you're good?"

I nodded, though he couldn't see me, realized that then murmured. "Yeah, I am. Nothing to do but wait this out and let the powers that be work their magic—or so I'm told."

"Seems wise."

"Plus, it's not a bad place to hide out."

"Live-in butler and giant pool?"

I glanced around the patio, saw the small sunken hot tub tucked into the corner of the greenery, thought about Tal cooking breakfast for me yesterday morning, me cooking for him last night. "More like a hot tub and a fully-stocked fridge."

Rob whistled slowly. "Living the dream, Conners. Living *the* dream."

I laughed, felt that prickling in my eyes again, touched that he'd cared enough to check up on me. "Rob?"

"Yeah?"

"Thanks—" I cleared my throat. "You know . . . for texting . . . no one else—"

I broke, stifling the rest of that before I admitted that my own flesh and blood hadn't so much as sent a text. Not that radio silence was something out of the ordinary with Mark. There was always an impenetrable wall between my older brother and myself, no matter how hard I tried to get through it.

Silence, this time one not filled with peace, not full of me daydreaming about clouds turning into animals.

It was long and quiet . . . and chock-full of awkwardness and embarrassment.

At least on my end.

"Tammy," Rob said eventually, not sounding the least bit discomfited. Instead, his words were tiny angry bullets, biting through the airwaves to reach my eardrums. "I don't mean to speak ill of the dead, but your dad was an asshole."

My lungs seized, air sliding out from between my lips in a long, slow hiss.

"He was," Rob added before I managed to summon anything further. "And your brother, I'm sorry to say, is taking a page right out of his book."

More seizing. More embarrassment sinking into my spine.

"You're a nice person, Tam. You always go the extra mile. You're kind and compassionate and a good officer." A beat. "They were and are too wound up in their own misery to see that."

Heart thudding in my chest, I whispered . . . something. Because, frankly, I wasn't even aware of the words coming out of my mouth.

"No, Tammy. It's not your fault."

I blinked, finally processed what I'd said.

It's my fault.

Was it possible to die of mortification? To just melt into the floor like a complete and utter weakling who completely lost my spine and any semblance of myself?

Unfortunately not.

"Okay." His voice took on a brisk tone. "So, I'm only going to say this once."

I waited, braced myself.

"Fuck them, Tam. You deserved better."

My fingertips were shaking, I realized obliquely, pressing them to my forehead and absorbing those words.

"You're right," I whispered.

Rob was quiet for a moment, and I heard the voices increasing in the background for a moment. "Glad you see it my way."

I snorted. "You're just loving that I said the male psyche's favorite phrase."

"You're right?"

"Yes, that."

We burst out laughing, and then Rob's daughter shouted something, and I knew I had to let him go. "Enjoy your family."

"Tammy?"

"Yeah?"

"Consider yourself on paid sick leave until otherwise cleared."

I frowned. "But I'm not sick." Media coverage couldn't be considered sick, right? Unless it was sick in the head.

"You have a knife wound in your arm, do you not?"

Well, there was that.

"Come back when you feel it's time," he said over the sound of a child's giggles. "We'll hold your place for you."

I thanked him, and we exchanged our goodbyes before hanging up, but I barely heard myself. Because all I could think was that Rob saying *we'll hold your place for you* might be the nicest thing anyone had ever said to me.

Because to have a place, somewhere I belonged . . .

It was what I'd always wanted.

"Why are you crying?"

I spun, not having heard Talbot come out.

"Why'd you sleep in the chair again?" I countered.

His lips twitched. "A question for a question?"

"Something like that," I murmured, wiping the tears that had finally emerged after all the stinging.

"I slept in the chair because I wanted to sleep in the bed."

I'd been studying the clouds again—a boa constrictor was floating over the hills—but his words brought my gaze back down. "What are you talking about?"

"I like you, Tammy," he murmured, closing the distance between us and stroking a finger down my cheek. "A lot."

"What does that have to do with you sleeping in a chair?"

"Everything."

That made no sense, and yet, it made perfect sense.

"I'm crying because, like a stupid idiot, I've finally realized that spending my life trying to find my value in everyone else— hoping *they* would see something I couldn't even see when I looked in the mirror—was a fucking waste of time." I threw my hands up, paced across the enclosed space. "It's so fucking lame because I've always wanted to belong, to be part of something, but I've never felt that I belonged, even to myself. And without that, how could I possibly hope to fit in anywhere else?"

More hot tears escaped, ones prompted by my past, my failures, my never finding what I wanted in other people. Because I had a giant hole inside me that would never be filled.

I was the key all along.

I lifted my chin, my gaze on the sky overhead. "It started with me," I whispered. "And it had to end with me."

I needed to fill that hole first.

I *had* to be the one, otherwise all the other pieces given to me by the wonderful people in my life—Maggie and Aaron, Rob and his wife, Melissa . . . Talbot—they would continue flowing out of me like sand flowing through an hourglass, drifting away into a useless pile that would then flow out all over again when the hourglass was turned over.

"My dad didn't give me what I needed after my mom died," I said, knowing Tal would hear it, knowing that he needed to hear it. "I searched for it in my brother, in other men, in my ex-husband, but it's in me. I'm the one who needs to find it."

A long stretch of quiet.

"I know exactly what you mean," he said, standing beside me. "This isn't me trying to take away from what you're saying, not at all. I just . . . I spent a long time trying to find my worth in other people, and that never felt good. It never felt like I could be completely happy because I was trying to absorb everyone else's feelings for me, instead of understanding my own."

Yes.

That.

I turned my head, studied his profile. "How did you find it in yourself?"

"Truth?" he asked, gold eyes coming to mine.

"Yes." I held his gaze. "Always the truth."

Emotion flickered across his face. "I can do that."

"Well?" I nudged his side with my elbow when he didn't immediately tell me. "What's that truth?" I asked.

"The truth is I'm still working on it," he said.

Which made me feel a whole lot less like a failure. "Yeah?"

He smiled that Hollywood smile, only this one had a touch of something I hadn't seen in his films, something that I was hoping very much was only for me. "Yeah." My lips turned up, and I focused back on the clouds.

An anteater. Another elephant. Or maybe a goose with a few extra feet.

"What are you doing?"

"Finding animals in the clouds," I said, matter-of-factly. "Well, that and trying to be happy and completely content with myself."

"So, small things."

I laughed.

"Come here."

"Where's here?" I asked suspiciously.

"What's it with you glaring at me in gardens?"

"I have no idea what you're talking about," I said innocently. "I'm just looking at four-footed geese transforming into adorable corgis."

"You've lost your mind," he said. "That isn't a corgi. It's a giraffe."

I gasped. "No freaking way. Look, there's her adorable heart-shaped butt and the long body with short legs."

Teasing gold eyes on mine. "I don't know what sky you're looking at—"

"Excuse me—"

He kissed me, hard and fierce and laced with affection.

And then I was in Talbot's arms, my back to his chest, his hands resting on my waist. "Tell me again where your mysterious corgi is," he murmured, the words a gentle whisper in my ear, his voice a heating pad on my stomach, easing the heavy pains on my insides. "I promise I won't be distracted looking at your ass again *or* be doing my level best to annoy you so you send those sexy, dark looks my way once more."

"You *what?*"

He nipped my earlobe. "You're glaring again."

"You can't even see my face."

"But I see you, beautiful. I. See. *You.*" Another nip. "And your *beautiful* glares."

I started laughing. He joined in.

And then I found a sense of belonging.

Only this time, it wasn't just from him, from another person, from his hold and his words and his body.

This time it was from me, too.

And that was pretty fucking great.

CHAPTER NINETEEN

Talbot

"WHAT'S a role you've taken that you wish you hadn't?"

I glanced over at Tammy, her arms resting over the edge of the hot tub. She was wearing a sports bra and a pair of my boxer briefs, and it was sexier than any bikini I'd ever seen.

Her head was tipped up to the sky again, though it wasn't bright and filled with clouds. It was clear, the temperature cool, and a multitude of stars twinkled overhead.

"Oof, that's a heavy list," I admitted.

Her gaze came to mine, amusement in the hazel depths. "I didn't mean it to be."

"I took any and every role I could when I was surviving on ramen noodles," I said, my lips curving. "And there were some bad ones."

"Including your role as the quintessential bad boy on the soap *Into Dreams*?"

I chuckled. "Including that one."

"Okay," she said, "so, which role since you've hit it big do you regret?"

"*Antonio.*"

Shock across her face, and I understood why. It was the first big film I'd shot, the one that had sent me into the world of celebrity. I'd had my pick of roles after that had come out, and I'd even gotten several awards shows honors.

"Why?" she asked, shifting on the built-in seat, and I noticed that the water was getting a little too close for comfort to her injury.

Sidling so that I was right next to her, I scooped her legs into my lap, propping her up so that her stitches were well out of the splash zone. "Because I was too new and insecure to do what I should have done with the role." I smoothed her hair back. "Antonio was a great character. He was strong and sensitive. He was critically flawed but managed to overcome his own bullshit in a way that wasn't contrite. If I'd known then what I do now about acting"—I shook my head—"I think it could have been so much better."

"Probably."

I blinked. "Ouch."

She smiled. "I didn't mean it like that."

"How *did* you mean it then?"

"Just that it's easy to look back and focus on all the ways we weren't perfect."

I continued stroking my fingers through her hair. "And what do you focus on that wasn't perfect?" I asked. "Because you seem pretty damned incredible to me."

She turned, glancing up at me, her lips so damned tempting that I had to taste her again—long and slow, with coaxing probes of my tongue. She tasted of the ice cream we'd had after dinner, chocolate and caramel with a dash of raspberry. It was from a local shop that made all their varieties in house, and it was absolutely delicious.

Doubly so when I got to taste it off her tongue.

"You're good at flattery," she murmured.

"Except, it's not flattery, Tammy, the savior of the dude in distress."

Her lips curved. "Dude in distress?"

I shrugged. "Is there a better damsel equivalent for men?"

She paused, tilted her head from side to side before resting it on my shoulder. "I suppose not. Yet another sexist form of the English language."

"How so?"

"There's no male word for whore, for bitch, for others," she said, lifting her glass of wine to her lips, "that I'm too blissfully relaxed to come up with at the moment. Damsel is another."

"Well, we should own it," I said, moving back to her hair, running my fingers through it again. "I'll gladly be the damsel in distress."

Tammy laughed before taking another sip. "So, *damsel* in distress, any other roles you don't like?"

"Nice try," I said, wanting to take advantage of her lounging against me all relaxed to find out more about her, about those scars and why she carried that heavy burden. I knew the outcome had become very much like mine—feeling empty and unfulfilled and yet with too much history of being hurt to easily put that aside—but I didn't know the why of it.

And with her on her second glass of wine, the tendrils of steam drifting off the surface of the water to gather on our skin, it seemed like as good a time as any.

"What do you mean?"

"I mean," I said. "You haven't told me about the things you look back on and regret."

"I'm regretting having this entire conversation," she muttered.

"We don't have to have it," I told her. "Let's talk more about the Milk Caper."

Relief in her eyes, though it was trailed almost instantly by determination. "No," she said. "That's not what I want to do. I just . . . my mom died when I was six. My dad fell apart. Hell, my family fell apart. We were three separate beings in a house, then two after my brother moved out. By the time I left for college, I don't think I spoke to my dad more than once a week, my brother even less." She sighed. "Though not for a lack of my trying. I wanted to—no, I was absolutely desperate for someone to connect with me, to come to my school plays or soccer practice, to take pictures of me before I left for a dance."

She went quiet for a long moment, and I struggled to find the patience to let her finish her story on her own terms.

"That's when I started finding all of those things I wanted in other people. Sad, huh?" she said, straightening, draping her arms back over the edge again. "My boyfriend at the time, his mom was the one to take the pictures. I played soccer for myself, for my team, no fans in the stands. I never got flowers after a play. Silly small stuff, you know?"

"Not silly."

A nod, her not contradicting me as she went on. "But it was also more than that. No home-cooked meals, no family time. When I was old enough, my dad gave me allowance to buy my own food, just like he did for my brother. We each had our shelves in the fridge, a cabinet with our purchases. We were like roommates." Tammy sighed. "It was hard after my mom died, having that change. But later, I adjusted, and . . . I just forgot, you know? And then I'd go to a friend's house and see how different it was—"

"And you'd remember all over again?"

"Yeah."

"Anyway, by the time my dad died, I was sad, but it was almost a relief. I didn't have to keep trying to make a place in his life for me."

"And your brother?"

Her smile was sad. "He's a product of the same system. How do you think it goes?"

I traced her palm with my fingers, her skin warm and damp. "I can imagine."

"I'm sure you can." Her hand twitched. "I think it's been six months since I've talked to him? I called him on his birthday, we spoke for two minutes, and that was it."

"And on your birthday? Does he call you?"

The pain in her eyes sliced me to the quick. I was a fucking idiot for having asked it in the first place.

"Never mind," I said, the words clipped out as rapidly as possible. "Let's talk about—"

She squeezed my hand. "I really am okay."

That smile she gave me did some squeezing of its own, grabbing my heart and clutching tightly. "Sweetheart—"

"You know what I want to do?"

"What's that?"

"I want . . ." A sigh, quiet as the breeze on a midsummer night rustling through grass, brushed along my spine. "I just want to stop looking backward and to just live my life."

"That sounds like sound advice."

"Either that or thrusting my head into the sand like an ostrich."

I squeezed her hand. "Don't do that."

"Do what?"

"Ostrich."

"Why do you care?" she asked archly.

I cared. I cared a whole freaking lot more than was reasonable for the short length of our friendship.

Not that I could tell her that.

Instead, I tugged a lock of her hair, the blond strand having escaped from her ponytail, and said, "I don't want that gorgeous face buried in the sand. Plus," I added. "How can I be a damsel in distress without you there to save me?"

She laughed, and fuck if that didn't make me feel ten feet tall. "Come on, damsel," she said, pushing out of the water. "Let's go inside before I turn into a prune."

I got out ahead of her, snagging our towels and then helping her down the steps.

"Tammy?" I asked as we walked toward the house.

"Yeah?"

"Any chance that the whole living-your-life thing involves me?"

Her lips curved, slow and sexy and full. "Yeah," she murmured. "I think there's a damned good chance of that."

CHAPTER TWENTY

Tammy

I STOPPED JUST before I stepped inside the house, not wanting my makeshift bathing suit to drip all over the floor.

"What is it?" Tal asked, his front coming very close to my back.

"The floor," I said by way of explanation.

He stepped in front of me. "What's wrong with the floor?"

I snorted, patted his cheek. "Sometimes, I forget I'm with a man who's spent his last years cloistered in a mansion with people to take care of his every whim."

"Hey! I resent that comment."

I gave him an arched look.

"Sometimes, it's a trailer and not a mansion."

Giggles bubbled out of my chest, and I shook my head at him. "I don't know how you can always make me laugh," I said. "But I'm glad for it."

Fingers on my cheek, a damp chest against mine. "Me, too."

Golden eyes, wide pupils, beautiful, long lashes.

"You're so fucking pretty," I said.

His cheeks went a little pink. "Tam—"

I dropped my towel.

Which was slightly less impactful since I was wearing a bra and his underwear, but the way his gaze dragged over my body, a nearly tangible scorch of heat, as though it were invisible fingers, made every inch of me jump to absolute rigid attention.

I wanted him.

Again.

Without all the angst.

"Tal?"

Those pretty gold eyes had landed somewhere in the vicinity of my breasts, and I glanced down, discovered why. My bra was plain white cotton, and the water had made it see-through.

Maybe I should be embarrassed that my breasts were on such blatant display, but aside from being completely over with the angst and insecurities, I was also absolutely and unequivocally attracted to this man. Seeing him look at me like that—heat in his eyes, his chest rising and falling in rapid succession, his cock hardened behind the closure of his swim trunks—I couldn't be insecure.

I just . . . wanted.

My fingers went to the waistband of the boxer briefs, and I started to push them down.

"No," he murmured. "Wait."

And then he scooped me up and carried me to the bed.

It was my turn to say, "Wait."

"No?" he asked.

"Not on the sheets," I said. "They'll get wet."

His smile was absolutely wicked, and I felt it right between my thighs, as though he'd thrust home and filled me to near-impossible proportions. Then he slowly released me, my body sliding down his, feeling every hard inch against me as my feet inched toward the floor.

Lips parting, breath trembling, I managed to not turn into a pile of goo.

Or not *too* much of one, anyway.

His fingers brushed back and forth above the waistband of the boxers, dipped beneath, the calloused length the sexiest roughness, especially when it became more than a finger, when both of his hands slipped beneath the sodden fabric to cup my ass and tug me toward him.

"Wet, huh?" A finger slid between my cheeks, the tip growing, gliding smoothly as he slid it forward and inside.

I moaned, the blunt intrusion making my knees buckle.

And then his hand was slipping free, the boxers were on the floor.

His lips found mine for a brief, blazing kiss. Then I was free again, my knees buckling again, my hips jerking, moans pouring out of my mouth as he bent, rucked up my bra, and sucked one of my nipples deep.

Pleasure flowed through me, filling me from my toes all the way out the top of my head. I scrabbled at his shoulders, trying to hold him closer, even as he pulled away, making me groan for an entirely different reason this time. I wanted more. I wanted him inside me and—

I reached for the tie of his swim trunks.

He brushed my hands away, reached for the drawer and pulled out a condom.

But I wasn't going to be deterred. I pushed him back a step, tugged open the fly, and pushed the shorts down. His cock sprang forward, and I gripped it tightly, dropping to my knees. "There you are, you glorious thing," I murmured, flicking my tongue over the blunt head, slipping it in between my lips to taste the salty skin.

Tal made a choking sound, his fingers tangling in my hair. "Baby," he murmured.

"Nope," I said, releasing him with a soft *pop*. "It's my turn to taste you now."

And I did just that, using my tongue to trace patterns up and down the hard length of him, wrapping my fingers around his cock, and stroking him firm and slow and sure. His hips jerked, curses poured out of his mouth, but I didn't let go, didn't stop until finally—

"Fuck!"

He tugged my mouth off, reached for me.

I let him tug my bra off because not only was it what I wanted, but it was something that was difficult with the wet fabric and my injured shoulder. As soon as it hit the floor with a sopping *thunk*, I pushed him back onto the mattress and climbed over him.

"Tammy," he began.

"No?" I asked, brushing my pussy over him, the scorching brand of him slipping between my folds.

"Yes," he groaned, head thrown back, the tendons of his neck standing out in sharp relief. "But—" His fingers dipped between my thighs, making me hiss out a breath, my thighs contracting around his.

"What?" I breathed.

"I needed to make sure you're ready."

It was my turn for a wicked smile. "Oh, I'm ready, baby." And I reached for the condom, rolled it on, and sank down onto him, my lips parting at that glorious pleasure pain of him pushing in, pressing deep, filling me plumb full. It was the freaking best, and almost too much, especially in this position. But Tal didn't move, just kept his hands on my hips, holding me in place, the hard thrust of him so freaking deep. "Tal?" I asked.

His fingers twitched, gaze locked on mine. "Hang on, Hazel Eyes. I need a second."

My hips flexed. He moaned. "To what?"

"To find some fucking control."

"Oh, no." I peeled his fingers from my hips, laced them with mine. "Oh, no, baby. We're not doing this thing with careful control." I writhed forward, pressing our interlocked hands over his head. "We're done with that bullshit." I nipped his throat, found his mouth for a kiss that sent my head spinning. "We're living this. Big and out loud and to our grandest potential."

Those gold eyes were blistering, scorching into my soul.

And then he flipped us, began stroking fast and furious, angling our hips so that he hit the absolute perfect spot. I was close in seconds, hurtling too fast, too rapidly for that edge.

But thankfully, he was right there with me, driving deep and steady, his face pulled into fierce, striking lines.

I moaned, tearing my gaze from his, unable to hold it as pleasure swarmed up and carried me over the edge, dragging me down the other side as he thrust several more times and froze, my name emerging from his lips, giving me the strength, somehow, to peel back my lids, and see the most beautiful sight I had ever seen.

A man staring down at me with affection, with need, with pleasure in his eyes.

Not just an orgasm.

But deeper, more meaningful.

"I see you, sweetheart," he murmured, lifting one hand to cup my cheek. "And we're going to see what we can do about filling each other's holes."

That was sweet.

So freaking sweet.

It was just also . . . so freaking bad.

I started laughing, my fingers finding his jaw, tracing through the bristles. "Filling holes indeed, you wonderful man."

Pink on his cheeks.

Affection in his eyes.

Then he started laughing, and it was the absolute best sound I'd ever heard.

———

THE NEXT MORNING, I was in the arms of a warm, snuggly Talbot, and I didn't want to ever get up.

But nature called.

So, I was required to slip from Tal's arms, out from beneath the cozy blankets, off the comfortable mattress, and pad across the floor until I reached the bathroom.

I did my business, took care of my ablutions, and then pawed my way through his drawers until I found one of his T-shirts, tugging it over my head. Then I did some more padding, this time past the temptation in bed and down the hall to the kitchen. I was starving, and I knew that he was going to wake up the same.

We'd worked up quite an appetite the night before.

Giggling, I walked into the kitchen.

And then did a very un-cop-like thing.

I screamed.

The man in the kitchen spun toward me, raising—I reacted without thinking, my body seeking cover, moving to put a wall between myself and the intruder before I fully processed what he held—a camera, pointed in my direction.

Pounding footsteps—from in front and behind.

Then Tal was there, putting himself between me and the man, the camera. I don't know why I was frozen, why I should have been reduced to a piece of furniture when I could take on an attacker with a knife, drag down a suspect, keep my head clear in any multitude of stressful situations.

But this one—a strange man, creeping toward me, a camera pointed in my direction, especially when I was naked beneath Tal's T-shirt—well, it had me reduced to a lump.

The shutter seemed gunshot loud, whirling *clicks* radiating about the space like bullets, gouging the peace and quiet by bouncing off the floor, the cabinets, the ceiling. My eyes drifted around, half-expecting to see gouges in the wood of the cupboards, chips out of the tile, holes in the sheetrock overhead. But . . . nothing was different.

Except, me.

"Get the fuck out of my house," Talbot growled.

The *clicks* didn't stop, even as the intruder said, "Come on, man. I'm just trying to—"

"You know you can't use those pictures," Tal said, still standing between me and the cameraman, shifting as the man came closer. "You're trespassing."

"I take 'em, someone will buy them. That's just the way it is." He walked toward us, still clicking away, the fucker, and I finally got my head out of my ass enough to actually be a part of this conversation.

I stuck my head out from behind Tal's shoulder. "Look you—"

"Tammy," Tal said. "Can you please walk to the panel there and hit the code six-four-seven-two?"

I blinked.

But despite being more than used to giving the orders, his tone had me instantly obeying. I moved to the keypad, punched in the numbers. Crossed back to Tal.

"Thank you," he murmured.

The paparazzo was moving around the room, his camera still pointed at us, at me, at Talbot. It was the most unnerving thing I'd ever experienced, even more so because of how casual he was, just walking around in a home that wasn't his, taking pictures in a constant fury.

"You need to leave," Tal said.

"I just need—" The camera dropped, and I saw the greedy look in his dark brown eyes, the shadows beneath, the lines around his mouth. He smelled like cigarettes, the odor filling the room, masking the lovely spice of Tal's scent. I hated that, hated the man who'd destroyed the small slice of peace, of happy we'd managed to build.

It was as though he had jabbed his fingers into the wound on my arm, was jiggling them around, just for good measure.

"He asked you to leave," I said. "And as an officer of the law—"

The front door burst open.

Two huge guys launched themselves at the intruder, and in approximately one-point-five seconds, he was face-first on the floor, his camera ripped out of his hands, and those hands restrained behind his back.

Talbot turned to face me, one hand on my uninjured arm, the other on my cheek. "God, Tammy, are you okay?"

"I'm fine."

He stared deeply into my eyes, and I saw regret pass through his. "I'm sorry."

I opened my mouth, ready to tell him that it wasn't his fault, but he was already turning back to face the trio of men.

"My camera!" the man complained.

One of the security guards shoved him more firmly into the floor, told him to "Shut the fuck up."

The other came over to us. "The police are on their way." He held up the camera. "I think you'll find that the camera's memory card is mysteriously wiped."

Tal nodded. "How'd he get in?"

Fury on the tall, built man's face. "I don't know that yet, Mr. Green. We'll review the tapes and—"

"I want Annalise here," Tal said in a voice harder than anything I'd heard before.

"I'm not sure—"

I could have sworn I heard Talbot's teeth grind together. "You tell your boss to get her ass down here immediately. I don't give a fuck where on the planet she is, but I expect her to be here by tonight." He stopped, shoulders rising and falling on a breath. "I don't pay through the fucking nose," he said quietly, fingers coming to the bridge of his nose and squeezing, "for a man to stab my woman in front of my house, for another to assault her in my house—"

I shivered—though probably not for the reasons he thought.

He still noticed, anyway. Though he didn't spare me a look as he wound an arm around my waist and hauled me to his side.

My shivering was two-fold. One, because he'd called me his woman, and two, because he was upset that I was the one affected—*stab my woman, assault her in my house*. I'd never had anyone ever think of me first, of the way that I'd been impacted by a situation, rather than themselves. It was just . . . unfathomable.

And I just . . . I just really liked it.

"I know, Mr. Green."

"Then get Annalise here," he gritted. "Get more help to secure the house. I don't care if you have to sleep on the fucking couch until I get the rest of it sorted."

"What sorted?" I asked.

He glanced out the window. "Until I find us a different place to stay."

"We've called in more teams," the guard said. "Once the police take this asshole away, two of us will always be in the house."

Talbot nodded then turned us in the direction of the bedroom when the sound of sirens filled the air. "We're getting dressed."

"I'll take care of the police until you're ready."

CHAPTER TWENTY-ONE

Talbot

I was furious with the people who were supposed to have been protecting her, and Tammy was making them meatloaf.

Well, at the moment, she was wiping her eyes because she was grating an onion into a bowl, having already rebuffed my attempts to help her, ordering me to grab one of those beers and to stop glowering at everyone until the alcohol content in the beverage quote, "Chills you the fuck out."

But there wasn't much that would chill me out.

I was absolutely furious, beyond fucking angry that someone would come into my house, that he'd scared Tammy—Tammy, who'd fucking fought off a knifed-attacker with hardly a fuss, and Tammy who'd screamed like . . .

Well, I don't think I'll forget the terror in that scream for a long, long time.

She swiped at her eyes again, and I set down my beer, crossed over to her, snagging a tissue from the boxes and dabbing at the stream of tears. "Why in the hell are you grating an onion?" I muttered, nudging her away from the bowl and taking over the task myself.

"Because it makes the meatloaf better," she said, moving to the sink and washing her hands.

"It can't possibly be worth it," I grumbled, scraping the onion up and down the metal surface.

"That's because you haven't eaten my meatloaf."

Since that was true, I didn't bother replying, just kept grating, even as I listened to Annalise coordinate with the security team in the other room. More guards would be staying in the house, which I fucking hated, but I also couldn't disagree with it. My realtor had managed to speed up closing for the house I'd bought, one that was much harder for people and paparazzi— and yes, after that morning, I was separating the two—to come anywhere close. There would be no more pictures in the driveway or shots of anyone on my porch. It was secure and would be wired with a state-of-the-art security system and staffed by guards who wouldn't miss something—

Like a fucking man breaking into my fucking kitchen.

"You're going to grate your fingers if you keep that up," Tammy murmured, taking the metal contraption and the dredges of the onion from my hand before nudging me out of the way this time. "I didn't think that you would be the type of person to get all broody."

"You were scared," I said.

That was more than enough reason for the brood.

"Yeah," she said, wincing. "Don't rub it in." A shudder. "I can't believe I screamed like that. It was just a freaking man with a camera, and I—" She shook her head. "The guys are going to give me so much shit."

And here she was, making jokes, cooking, totally not upset with the guards. In fact, she'd just said, "Sometimes things go wrong," and had shrugged.

Shrugged!

Meanwhile, I was reliving that scream, a bundle of jagged thumbtacks, each stabbing into me repeatedly as I remembered the terror I'd felt in hearing it.

"They do," I said, "and they'll answer to me."

Tammy turned, her hands still mixing in the bowl. "God, they'd give me shit for that, too." She rose on tiptoe, brushed her lips over mine. "But I'll still enjoy every moment of it."

I wanted another kiss.

This one deeper and longer and more intense than the peck.

I *wanted* to take Tammy back to the bedroom, after I kicked everyone out of the house, and spend the evening with her showing her how much she meant to me.

But she just shooed me away again, and so I went back to brooding over my beer, and knowing that I couldn't send anyone away, not when they were the means to keeping the woman who held my heart safe.

Maggie, who'd shown up about thirty minutes after the police, appeared in the kitchen and took one look at my face before tugging me close and hugging me tight. "Thank you," she whispered into my ear. She stepped back, rested a hip against the table.

"For what?"

She squeezed my hand. "For caring."

My eyes had drifted to Tammy as she worked, looking completely relaxed and unperturbed despite the events, despite the influx of people in the house. She was fucking incredible, and I didn't know how anyone would have a hard time caring for her.

She was . . . well, she didn't just hold my heart. She *was* my heart.

It had happened in a split second, my draw to her—sharp words, instant chemistry, a striptease trailed by a gun—and my falling deep had happened just as fast. A body shielding me, focused not on herself afterward, quiet competence and strength and courage.

The night before had tugged me further down the rabbit hole, and the scream this morning, knowing how quickly a life could be snuffed out . . .

One injection too many.

A knife sailing through the air.

One scream.

And I'd known that I was in love with Tammy Conners.

She was both exactly like me and completely different. She was strong and smart and had a giant heart. She'd been hurt, sometimes she replied with barbs when things got too scary, but she'd also met me more than halfway with sharing the painful things about her past.

And I knew there wasn't another woman I could be with who would understand that inner pain so precisely, who knew what it was like to long for something and long and *long* and to always be left empty and wanting.

I hadn't found someone before her because they couldn't know what that was like.

But Tammy did.

Which meant that she understood exactly what it took for me to let her in.

And I understood right back.

I stood up, brushed past Maggie, barely aware enough to offer a half-apology for my abruptness.

Then I was across the room, taking Tammy in my arms.

She pushed against my chest. "Tal," she began, laughing lightly. "I need to—"

I kissed her.

Deep, as though by taking her mouth, feeling her lips on mine, my tongue dipping into her mouth, that I could imprint her onto my soul. That if only I kissed her long enough, held her tight enough that I'd always be able to feel her on my skin.

Only when my lungs were screaming for air did I manage to tear myself away. I cupped her cheek.

"I love you," I whispered.

She froze, glanced at me then down to her hands. "I—I—" A sharp shake of her head. "I ruined your shirt."

My gaze dropped to my shirt, saw that it had been smeared

with raw meat. "I don't care." I tilted her head back up, stared into those beautiful hazel eyes, and said again, "I love you."

Her pupils dilated; her lips parted.

I felt her breath on my skin.

"B-but . . . *how?*"

I pulled her a little closer. "But how could I not?" I said, and then I kissed her again, ignoring the voices in the front room, finally able to halt the rending that was tearing through me over what had happened to her because of me. Finally able to quiet the voices in my head and just be with her in this moment.

"Tal," she whispered. "I—I—"

"Shh," I said. "I don't need you to say it back. I don't need you to say *anything*. It's in my heart, and it's without strings. I love you, Hazel Eyes, and I'm not letting you go."

Her throat worked as she swallowed several times.

Then, abruptly, she pushed against my chest, not gently, but firmly. "Let me go," she said. "Let me—"

Heart sinking, I dropped my arms.

She turned away, and I watched as she walked to the sink and washed her hands, scrubbing fiercely and rapidly. I braced myself as she spun back to face me, her eyes flashing.

"How *dare* you?" She poked a finger into my chest, finding a bit of non-meat-covered fabric and pressing it into my skin.

I understood that part wasn't pertinent.

But it was easier to process than the disappointment coursing through me at her tone, at the fury on her face.

"How dare you?" she said again, the question short and clipped and—

Her hands came to my jaw and she yanked my head down, kissing me until my body was on fire, until my lungs were desperate for air, until my brain was hazed with the fog of desire. I could feel only Tammy. I didn't care one bit about my dirty shirt or the burning in my lungs. I could survive on just this woman's kisses, and her kisses alone.

"How *dare* you?" she said for a third time, finally pulling her mouth free and staring deeply into my eyes. Her fingers didn't move from my cheeks, just held me in place as she finished, "tell me that you love me when I couldn't hold you without risking giving you salmonella?"

Her lips curved.

My heart stuttered and stopped.

"As insane as this is," she whispered, "considering I've known you only for a few freaking days."

My lungs froze.

"I love you, too, Tal," she whispered. "I don't know how—" A shake of her head. "No," she said, more firmly. "I *know* how." Her hands tightened on my face. "It's because you showed me who you were, you showed me that *I* could be important to someone, you showed me that I could find that importance in myself." She smiled. "Maybe I would have gotten there eventually, but you—"

"I what?"

"You're wonderful."

My heart thudded against my ribs.

"Just—" Her lips twitched again, and I felt that smile in my soul. "You're just absolutely wonderful, baby."

Her lips found mine.

And I forgot about the other people in the house. I scooped her up, carried her down the hall, and dropped her into bed.

"The meatloaf," she murmured.

I ripped off my dirty shirt, tugged hers off as well, throwing both to the floor. "They can order in."

CHAPTER TWENTY-TWO

Tammy

THIS TIME when I walked into the kitchen, after the sun glaring in through the windows again woke me, I wasn't surprised to see the man standing by the coffee pot.

I wasn't thrilled to see him, however.

Especially, since Talbot had carried me off to bed, and we hadn't emerged for dinner. A fact that every one of the security guards would certainly know.

"Morning," I whispered as he poured himself a cup of coffee.

"Morning." He held up the pot.

I nodded.

He filled me a mug while I went to the fridge, searching out something for breakfast and finding that someone had wrapped up my meatloaf components. Which was just as well. I could make it tonight.

My phone buzzed, and I pulled it from the pocket of my leggings, saw that it was Maggie calling.

"Hey," I said, swiping and putting it up to my ear.

"How's the throat?"

"I—uh—what?" I asked, closing the fridge and moving to grab the mug. The security guard had already left the room, so I had free reign as I surveyed the rest of the kitchen.

"Never mind."

"No," I said, grabbing a banana out of the basket. "What is it?"

Maggie chuckled. "I'm just being an asshole because we all heard how very happy Talbot made you last night."

It took me a second.

And then it took me too freaking long to melt into the floor.

Because it didn't happen.

Ugh.

"See?" Maggie said. "Asshole."

I made a face. "Yes, you are."

She giggled, and I found myself smiling and shaking my head. "Asshole-ness aside, you're a good friend, Mags."

"Because I have an in with sexy-as-shit actors who can give you copious amounts of happy times?"

"Yes, *that*," I said, still smiling as I sipped my coffee. "And also because you give a damn about me. You always have."

Mags was quiet. "I wish I hadn't lost contact with you when I left town."

My friend had a similar upbringing, a tough childhood and not a lot of support, outside of Aaron. But they'd been boyfriend and girlfriend in high school, and far too young to settle down. So Mags had left to pursue her dream of living a big life—which she'd found, of course, in Talbot, Pierce, Artie, and recently in a second chance with Aaron. Still, that big life had meant things had gotten left behind, especially since it wasn't nearly so easy to communicate then as it was now.

We'd reconnected by chance, and now . . . I had my friend back.

"We were all too young and stupid to look that far ahead," I said. "I'm just glad we're back in each other's lives now."

"Even though it's brought you into a media frenzy."

"I still don't like my face on all those papers and posts," I said, "but my life with you and Tal in it is infinitely better than without you."

"Flatterer."

"Yup," I teased. "Everything I feel about you and our friendship is a joke."

"If I was there, I would swat you."

"Speaking of that," I said. "Why *aren't* you here? Are we not having our daily crisis meeting of the minds?"

"Actually, no," she told me. "We don't need that today."

I slurped down more coffee. "Why?"

"Because word got out about the intruder, and the public isn't happy. They're boycotting any images of you and Talbot." She laughed. "You guys even have your own hashtag."

My brows were practically in my hairline. "A hashtag?"

"Yup. Hashtag FreeTalmy."

"Um, what?"

"It's your couple name," she said. "Talbot and Tammy equals Talmy."

"That's . . . "

"Super, ridiculously cool?"

"No," I said, wrinkling my nose. "It sounds like the brand for a tampon."

Maggie hooted with laughter, and I found myself unable to stop the giggles. "Talmy," I breathed, plunking down my mug. "How is that a thing?"

A warm arm slipped around my waist. "How is *what* a thing?"

I was still laughing as he hauled me up, didn't protest when he snagged my cell from my hand and put it on speaker. "How is *what* a thing?" he asked again.

Maggie got control of herself much sooner than I did.

"You two have a hashtag," she said, still chuckling. "And a couple name."

His eyes came to mine, brows drawing together. "Tell me you are not serious," he said.

"I think you'll find that you like being part of a couple name," Maggie said, her voice filled with teasing. "I've already filed for the trademark and am setting up a website for merch and—"

My jaw fell open. "You *didn't*."

More laughter, though this time, it wasn't paired with laughter of my own. "Of course, I didn't," she said, "but it is good news." She went on to explain about the hashtag and photo boycott, how the paparazzo had been booked on charges of criminal trespassing and had apparently been exiled from the group of camera-toting men and women outside the gate. "There are even fans outside with homemade signs emblazoned with *Free Talmy.*"

Tal pulled up the feed on his cell, and we both stared, dumb-struck at the line of people with neon-colored posterboards blocking the paparazzi.

"Free Talmy, Free Talmy," Mags chanted lightly. "It has a ring to it."

I shuddered again at the name but felt inexorably touched by the gesture. "Yeah," I said, "it has a ring to it, if you're a whale."

Talbot snorted, setting his cell aside. "So, we'll be free of this mess soon?"

I moved to the fridge, started getting out ingredients. I could feel his gaze on me, but I just kept gathering what I needed, setting the eggs, milk, and butter on the counter then moving to the pantry for flour, baking soda, and sugar. Oh, and chocolate chips. Couldn't forget the chocolate chips.

"I think it would be prudent to make a statement and maybe include a picture of you two on your Instagram and Facebook pages, especially since you two are together now." A beat. "You are together, aren't you?"

"I don't know about Mr. Green," I said lightly. "But I'm just here for the hot sex."

Mags made a retching sound.

"Don't even," I said, pulling out a bowl and starting to measure ingredients. "I had to hear *all* about your hillside romp with Aaron in Tuscany, so you can certainly deal with a bit of my happy times with Talbot."

"What are you doing?" the man in question asked.

"I'm making cookies."

He glanced at the clock. "It's seven-thirty in the morning."

"And?" I raised my brows.

"And . . . nothing, I guess," he said.

"*What's* happening?" Mag asked, her voice slightly tinny through the speakerphone.

"Tammy's making cookies."

"Maybe I *do* need to come over for our mid-morning emergency meeting."

"Maybe, you do," I called, cracking several eggs into the bowl. "It's your recipe."

Mag sighed. "You play mean, Conners. I'm curled up with my fiancé, and you're tempting me out of my nice cozy bed."

"Well, by the time you pried yourself out and made it through traffic, I doubt there would be any left."

"Why?"

"Because I'm making them for the *Free Talmy* people out front."

Talbot froze, his face a comical mask, shock written across every pretty line.

Silence from him . . . and from the call on my cell.

Then Maggie started chortling, right around the time I began mixing in chocolate chips.

"What?" Tal and I asked at the same time.

"She's good, Tal. She is good."

I frowned. "What do you mean?"

"Ignore me," Mags said. "Deliver the homemade cookies. Just bring a security guard with you."

"I don't think that's necessary—"

"It is," Tal said.

"Yes," Mags added. "Listen to your big sexy man."

"She's glaring at you now," Tal stage whispered.

"She's scary when she does that," Mags whispered back.

I sighed. "I'm going to have to watch it with you two."

"She's got angry eyes," Tal said.

"Ooh, extra scary."

I snorted, tried to hold on to those angry eyes, but I couldn't do it. Not with these two jokers teasing me, not with the love I felt for both of them in my heart. "I'm ignoring you," I said, scrounging until I found a cookie sheet and beginning to scoop out the dough, and since I didn't do this quietly, it wasn't long before Tal slipped into the other room to chat about business things instead of teasing me about my scowling.

Which was just as well.

Without interruptions, I quickly got the cookies in the oven, and soon the house smelled like sugar and butter and chocolate.

The best smell ever.

Luckily, I made a double batch (with my years on the force, I wasn't stupid about how much junk food humans, especially those at work, could fill their stomachs with), and before long, I had security team members drifting into the kitchen, looking longingly at the cookies cooling on the racks.

I parceled them out, giving plenty to the guards with the longing eyes, and the rest I put on a platter before grabbing a stack of napkins.

Poking my head into the other room, I held up the tray as I met Tal's eyes.

He was still on the phone, although he'd switched cells, since mine was on the coffee table, and it sounded like he was also no longer talking to Mag, since his tone was far more serious and the conversation far more involved. Slipping out, I grabbed one of my cookie-bribed guards to watch my back, made sure I was fully dressed—no more pants-less pictures please—and headed out the front door.

The first thing that surprised me was the noise.

I'd been inside so much, and outside only in that small, secluded garden, that I hadn't realized the baseline amount of noise a crowd of people made. Noise that increased in volume when the remaining paparazzi spotted me, lifting their cameras, that strange *whirring* of their shutters clicking filling the air.

Then the voices joined in—a hum turning into a drone, excitement drifting up from the gate.

I strode down the long driveway toward the crowd, thinking this was probably exceptionally stupid, even if Mags and Talbot hadn't vetoed the idea. Still, I thought it was sweet that they were protecting Tal, and by extension, me, and I knew how much a small gesture like this could make a person feel wanted.

And that, more than anything of these last couple of days, was the thing I wanted to take away from this experience the most.

Care didn't have to have strings.

Care didn't need to be grand and overt.

Care could be an omelet in the morning, chicken parmesan in the evening. It could be searching cabinets for "girl shit," just as easily as it could be standing in front of a person invading our space.

The little things were those that I had been missing for so long. Those were the things Tal gave me.

And those were the things that I was going to give back to the rest of the world.

I wanted those people who didn't have those little things, the quiet joy, to have them from me, even if they were just cookies warm from the oven and a quiet thanks.

"There's a lot of people," I whispered, feeling my steps slow unbidden. This had all seemed so easy in the house. Just bring cookies to the nice people outside. They'd appreciate the thought, and it would make us both feel good.

That was true.

What was also true?

There were a *lot* of eyes currently watching me navigate my way barefoot down the driveway, not a stitch of makeup on, my legs in black sweats, my torso covered in a bulky hoodie of Tal's.

It wasn't exactly glamorous.

It probably wasn't another image I wanted plastered everywhere.

"Shit," I whispered.

"I'm here," the guard, whose name was Tex, said. "And we already have back up positioned by the gate."

"Right," I said. "So, I'll try to pretend this isn't terrifying because you guys won't let anything happen to me." And not that it was just occurring to me exactly what dating Tal would be like. People staring. More pictures—and probably unflattering ones at that, because I wasn't going to stop wearing hoodies and leggings—gracing covers and blog posts.

He was worth it.

I felt that in my gut, without a doubt.

But this was also a lot for any normal woman to deal with.

Tex chuckled. "Oh, it's not terrifying because of your safety." I glanced up, met his dancing eyes. "You forget, I saw how you handled yourself in that video."

I made a face. "But they still have my gun."

Another chuckle. "You'll be fine." His voice dropped. "And I'm fully aware that it's terrifying because that's a shit-ton of people looking at you."

Yup. *That* was what was terrifying.

"You're not helping."

"You got this," he said, giving me the slightest nudge forward.

I clenched the platter tighter, lifted my chin. "Of course, I do."

"That's the spirit."

"Tammy!"

I blinked, somehow surprised they knew my name when I really shouldn't be, not when we had a hashtag and a couple name, but it was an otherworldly experience for a grown woman to just be shouting my name.

And then other voices rang out, joining the first.

Calling my name, asking where Talbot was, if we were all right. The paparazzi were shouting, too. Telling me to smile or to look here or there. I did my best to ignore the cameras and walked to the woman who first called my name. "Hi," I said through the gate. "I'm Tammy."

She smiled. "I know your name," she said, and I could have smacked myself. Oh, of course she knew it. She just called out to me. "I'm Mary."

"Nice to meet you," I murmured then stalled out for several awkward moments until I lifted the tray. "Well . . . I just want to thank you for your kindness, so I . . . um . . . if you like, I baked some chocolate chip cookies. They're nut-free, but they have eggs and dairy."

Her brows drew together. "You baked them? For us?"

I felt my cheeks go pink. "Um . . ." I nodded. "Yeah, I— They're still warm from the oven."

"Oh."

I held up the napkins.

Her face lit up as she reached for one of the paper squares and used it to pick up a cookie through the gate. It was silly and a little difficult, but we managed.

Then she took a bite . . .

And as I moved on to the next person, spending a couple of moments talking to them, maneuvering them another cookie, I knew this was right.

Show that care I'd missed out on, that I'd longed for, to others.

Without expecting anything back. Without strings and expectations because in the process of that giving, their smiles, their words, the blips of happiness on their faces filled me up in a way that I hadn't even known was possible.

And I knew that even though my life had taken a sharp right turn over the last few days, I would be just fine.

CHAPTER TWENTY-THREE

Talbot

I HELD a file in my hands and a whirlwind of butterflies in my stomach.

It had been a week since Tammy had wooed the crowd in front of the gate with her homemade cookies—a recipe Maggie had giddily shared on my Instagram, along with a snap of those fresh-baked circles of goodness I'd taken before they'd all disappeared. The crowd had mostly gone at this point, only a handful of paparazzi still camped out front.

But I didn't care.

One, because we'd snuck out in the dead of night to my new house hidden in the hills a good distance away.

And two, because this house didn't have any clear lines of sight for cameras, *and* Tammy had reviewed the security procedures with the team. There wasn't anything sexier than a woman stating words like "line of sight" (see? I learned that one from her) and "backup security rounds" (I liked *her* rounds, ha) and "patrol the perimeter" (which was just fun because of the alliteration—patrol perimeter, patrol perimeter, *patrol perimeter*).

But the point was that she felt comfortable, *I* felt comfortable, and we were able to live together without the intrusion of cameras.

It was like the best first date ever. And also the longest.

Which was fine with me. I didn't want the date to end. I wanted it to go on and on and on, to never stop and . . . that brought me to the folder in my hand. The one I needed to show Tammy because I was set to leave to shoot my next film in a little over a week, and she was readying to return home. Our longest, best first date had an end date, and as much as I loved hanging out and cooking together and having lots of glorious sex, I wanted to make sure that we had plans in place so that our long, best first date could continue indefinitely.

"There!" she said, triumphantly placing the square on the board.

She had surprisingly nerdy taste in board games. Which was fine with me. I had quite a collection of board games, especially the nerdy ones—though we'd had to open up quite a few boxes in order to locate the one she'd wanted to play tonight. Prior to meeting Tammy, most of my stuff had already been in storage in anticipation of my move, all except for my bedroom and kitchen. Those had been packed and moved over right along with us in the middle of the night by a scarily organized woman and her very effective crew.

Now I glanced down at the pieces Tammy had played and knew that I'd met my match.

"Two dungeons *and* four unique pieces on either side," she crowed, doing a happy little dance. "Beat that."

There was no way I could beat that.

"I yield, oh dragon master," I said, pushing the board away from me and fiddling with the folder in my lap again.

"You going to show me that?"

"What?" I glanced up from the table to her eyes, which were filled with warmth.

"Whatever you're fondling in your lap," she said. "Either that, or you're fondling something else, and I don't know whether I should be sad to be left out of the fun or disgusted."

"Disgusted," I quipped. "Definitely disgusted."

She laughed quietly then began stacking pieces, not bothering to tally up the score because one look at our respective boards told even the most casual viewer that she had absolutely obliterated me.

Once they'd been cleared, she looked at me expectantly.

I handed her the folder.

Her brows drew together, a slight V forming between them.

I opened it. "I was thinking . . ."

"What is this?" she breathed.

"I was thinking," I said again. "That I don't have much of a need to continue living in L.A. anymore. I have this place if I need to be here for work, but otherwise I'm either on set or . . . well, I want to be with you."

She glanced up from the listings of houses I'd had my realtor pull together. Houses that were located in Darlington, Utah.

Because my life might not be there, but Tammy's was.

"What is this?"

I'd broken her.

After pushing up from my seat, I rounded the table and crouched near her side. "Pick one," I said. "Or we can pick one together. But I don't care which house we live in—I just want to live in one with you." I cupped her cheek. "I want to be with you. I want to build a life together and have you make me cookies that don't all get eaten before I ate only a single, paltry one"—I gave her sad, puppy eyes, which had her smiling, the shock wearing off her expression—"I know things have moved so fast, that we've been living in this alternate reality with forced proximity and dangerous situations. I just want to have a chance for us to be us together."

She softened, shifting in her seat to face me. "But will there be board games?"

"For you to destroy me in them?"

A smirk. "Naturally."

I nodded. "There will be board games."

"And omelets?"

I took her hand. "And omelets. And," I whispered, leaning very close. "If you're very, *very* good, I'll even make you my special blueberry pancakes."

She leaned in, her lips coming to my ear. "Blueberries are my favorite."

"Are they now?" I asked, turning my head so that our mouths were suddenly perfectly aligned.

A nod.

"Well, then," I said. "I guess you'd better pick a house."

"Tal?"

"Hmm?" I asked, having gotten distracted by the column of her throat and starting to kiss my way down it.

"It's just . . . I'd rather we stay at my house," she whispered. "It's on the edge of town and isolated. We could put in some security protocols, but Darlington is safe and—"

I placed my finger over her lips. "Tammy?"

It was her turn to murmur, "Hmm?"

"I'd love that."

"Really?" she asked, after peeling my finger back. "It's not fancy like this place and—"

"I don't need fancy," I said. "I just need you."

Her smile was bright enough to light up the world, and I knew that even though we were just starting out, that we were going to be okay.

———

TAMMY WAS ASLEEP IN BED, and I was answering emails.

Did that still constitute us being on our long, best first date?

Maybe?

Despite us separating at intervals throughout the day, we

always found each other at small, random moments. Me stroking my fingers down her neck as she talked with her boss about what her schedule would look like when she returned, her squeezing my shoulder as I squinted over offers that Mags sent over. Me bringing her some of that sludge while she relaxed on the back patio. Her finding out that my favorite meal was Pad Thai and finding a recipe so she could cook it for me. Board games at noon, movies in the evening. It felt like every minute was completely full of a life I hadn't known was possible, and also as though I were on the most incredible vacation of my life.

Apart and yet not. Finally belonging for the first time ever.

I was part of a pair.

And it felt fucking great.

I was feeling great, better than I'd ever felt in my life. In fact, I was feeling so great that I was going to close my laptop, cuddle up with my woman, and go to bed at the very "late" hour of ten P.M.

Ha.

We'd had an eventful couple of weeks, okay?

Plus, that afternoon, Tammy had her stitches taken out, after which we'd gorged on homemade pizza, watched a movie, and then my woman had crashed.

And she was beautiful when she slept.

Too beautiful and peaceful for me to keep scrolling through tedious emails on my laptop. I closed the lid, set it on the nightstand, then did what I should have done in the first place: I gathered her in my arms, held her close, and let sleep carry me under.

My phone rang, what felt like minutes later, and I released Tammy, sitting up and seeing that it wasn't mere minutes past when I'd lain down. It had been just over an hour, and when my eyes flicked to the caller ID, seeing that Maggie was calling, I felt my stomach knot.

The peace of the last week was over.

I knew that in my fucking bones.

Mentally cursing, I slipped out from beneath the blankets and lifted my phone to my ear the moment I was in the hall.

"Mags?" I asked. "Is everything okay?"

"No, Tal," she said. "It isn't."

And that was when the bottom fell out of my world.

CHAPTER TWENTY-FOUR

Tammy

I'D DISTANTLY HEARD the phone ring, felt Tal get out of bed—and it was funny, in the best possible way—that my body was so in tune with his I didn't for one moment question where I was when I woke with him curved around me.

These last two weeks—with the exception of the whole assault, media frenzy, and home invasion—had been the absolute best of my life.

Finding my rhythm with this man, learning everything and anything I could, and continuing to fall deeper and deeper until I felt as though I would never surface from the bliss. I knew I would, of course. That was life, and we were two people who'd had tough upbringings, and it wasn't like either of us were short on the whole stubborn gene thing. But those tough childhoods and the stubbornness were assets when it came to this.

I'd known instantly that Tal was different.

He'd shown me that he'd thought I was different, too.

And though it had been particularly terrifying, we'd both leaped in with two feet.

There was something safe and secure about hurtling oneself

off a cliff—so long as the person who loved me and whom I loved right back held my hand as we plummeted down.

But now—I frowned, sat up—that man who was plunging down alongside me was talking hurriedly into the phone, his voice equal parts clipped and shocked and . . . I was already moving when I heard the crash.

I rushed into the hall, saw him on one knee, his head cradled in his hands.

The phone was on the floor, and I scooped it up. "Hello?"

"Tammy?"

Maggie's voice was frantic. "Look, I'm almost there," she said hurriedly.

"Here?" My stomach was twisting itself into knots.

"The hospital," she said.

"Oh, my God. Are you hurt?"

"No." A sharp breath. "Look, I'm sorry, I'm panicked here. I received a call from the hospital about the John Doe who attacked you guys. He's awake, and he apparently asked someone to put something online for him and—"

She broke off.

My pulse was a rapid tattoo in my veins, my lungs might as well have been pulling in carbon dioxide instead of air, but I managed to push out, "What?"

"He's saying he's Tal's father."

I nearly dropped the phone myself, realized obliquely that it had been the *thunk* I'd heard a few moments before. "You cannot be serious," I whispered.

"I know," she whispered back. "I'm meeting the police there. We'll get the nurse to take the video down, but"—a curse —"there are millions of views already. This story isn't going away, and it's not going to look good."

"He came at us with a knife," I pointed out.

"If he is Tal's dad."

My eyes slid closed and I said, "And the fact that he was shot and nearly killed by his son's girlfriend isn't a great look."

Mag's voice was brittle, sad laced into every syllable. "The optics aren't good, no."

I inhaled, exhaled, and carefully placed my hand on Tal's back. "Will the man consent to a DNA test?"

Tal stiffened.

I moved my palm in gentle circles.

"He's already provided a sample."

Tal moved so fast that I could hardly blink before the cell was out of my hand and pressed to his ear. "This is bullshit, Maggie. My father is dead of an overdose, in a gutter somewhere."

Whatever she said in response had his face falling.

I took the phone from his hand, put it on speaker.

"Maggie?" I said.

"I think Tal should give a sample, too" she said softly. "Not just because of this man, but for himself, because he's going to always wonder if he doesn't."

I thought she was right.

But I could also see Talbot's face, see the broken quality of his expression, and I knew that he wasn't going to be receptive to anything that was logical and sound at that moment. He'd had a giant shock. He was hurt. He was . . . wondering.

"We'll call you back," I murmured.

"Tammy?"

"Yeah, Mags?"

"Take care of him."

"That's never in doubt," I said and hung up. The resultant silence was very . . . well, it sounded stupid to say, but it was very quiet and heavy, a smothering thundercloud surrounding me, pressing on my lungs. "Tal," I began, when I could take the oppressive pressure no longer.

He burst to his feet in another of those quick, abrupt movements.

Then he was striding away from me.

"Tal!" I called.

He didn't stop, just walked down the hall and out the back door, not looking back, not saying a word, not even when I followed after him and called his name again. Not even as he disappeared into the dark of the property, well away from the lights of the house, becoming little more than a shadow that faded away to nothing after a few more moments.

"Fuck," I whispered.

I returned to the bedroom, threw on a pair of sweats and a hoodie, then grabbed my phone, shoved my feet into shoes, and followed him, skirting the pool, hurrying down the steps, moving in the direction I'd last seen that shadow disappearing.

The moon was high overhead, illuminating my path, but I didn't see Tal anywhere, not even when I used the flashlight on my cell to search the nearby area.

"Fuck," I whispered again—

And then I heard it.

A strange pounding sound.

Thunk. Thunk. Thunk.

I followed it, saw another shadow emerge, this time one that I recognized. It was Tex, my cookie assistant. Moving toward him, I stopped just to his side.

"You got him?" he asked.

"Yeah, thanks," I said. "Can you make sure we have some privacy?"

"Done." He stepped back, blended into the shadows.

And I followed the *thunk, thunk, thunk* to the man who'd stolen my heart in a matter of days—no, the man to whom I'd freely offered up my heart, and who'd offered his in return.

He'd stopped near one of the large oak trees on the property, its wide expanse of branches providing Tal with more shadows, more coverage from the moonlight above. It didn't take a genius to process what he was doing—punching the trunk. Over and over again, until I knew that his knuckles must be a bloody freaking mess.

I made my way over to him, staying well out of the way of his backswing as he threw his punches.

Stopping once I'd circled around to face him, the trunk between us, I waited, biting back my winces as the *thunking* continued, as my eyes slowly adjusted to the dark. He was like a demon possessed, the blows fast and furious, and I knew he was going to be hurting—although probably not as bad as what was tearing him up inside. Because that had been a thorn buried deep, one that had hurt him over and over again, one that was freshly uncovered and jabbing him once more.

Parents had the unique ability to wound their children repeatedly—through neglect and assault, through sharp words and insecurities prodded, and through what Tal and I had both dealt with, abandonment.

So, perhaps we'd begun filling in those gaps, the yawning, jagged crevices, but we would never be completely whole.

That option had been taken from us.

But I wasn't leaving him.

I could wait for him to get his fury out—barely. Hate that he needed to beat up a tree—and his hands—in order to do so, even as I understood the urge and wouldn't intervene for the moment. But I wasn't going to stand back and watch him suffer like this. I was going to take some of this fucking burden off his shoulders because I damn well knew that he would absolutely do the same for me.

Finally, he stopped punching, stepped back, chest heaving, head hanging, and I slipped between him and the trunk, taking his hands in mine.

Just as I'd suspected, they were beat up to hell.

He'd have realistically battered hands for his knight movie, I supposed, so long as he hadn't actually broken anything.

That would probably mess something up.

"You should have used your sword," I whispered.

Tal was frozen, silent for long moments. Then, "I didn't want to hurt the tree."

I pressed a kiss to a small patch of undamaged skin. "Baby, you hurt yourself."

"Good."

My temper spiked, my fingers clenching around his wrist. "No, you dumb ass," I snapped, and here I paused for a second, considered if I should go with the soft, gentle approach. I studied his face, saw the recalcitrance there, and realized this wasn't the time to go soft and gentle. This time, my care needed to be in the form of a woman who wasn't going to allow her man to sink down into the depths of despair.

"No," I said, my tone fierce. "You don't get to hurt yourself, not because something from your past might have come up, and not because someone struck out trying to wound you." I reached up, gripped his face. "If that man *is* your dad—and I'll admit that it gives me more than a blip of guilt to think that I might have shot the person who fathered you—"

His face gentled.

And no, he didn't get to do that either, didn't get to turn this onto me, to try and ease my conscience.

I kissed him—hard and deep—then stared intently into his eyes. "If that man is truly your father, then you'll have closure, baby. You'll know what happened, and you can put it behind you. Because"—and here, I jostled him lightly—"even if he is your freaking sperm donor, the truth is from what you've told me, he never was a dad to you."

Tal inhaled sharply.

"So this man, who tried to harm you, who might have harmed you when you were a child, is a fucking monster, and he doesn't deserve a thing from you." I slid one hand down, rested it over his chest. "But you," I whispered. "You deserve more, and if there is even a small part of you hidden down deep inside, then you deserve to know whether or not what he's saying is the truth."

Quiet.

Long, tense, stifling silence again.

Tal going so still, I could hardly see him breathe.

Then he pulled out of my arms, spun away, and strode off.

Despair curled inside me as I watched him go, hating that I'd clearly said the wrong thing, that I'd snapped at him. I should have gone with soft and gentle, should have comforted and been—

Warm arms wrapped around me, hauling me against a hard chest.

"You're right, Hazel Eyes," he whispered into my ear.

Every nerve ending inside me relaxed, my body spinning in his, pressing my front to his. "About so many things," I said lightly, so freaking relieved that he'd circled back around, that I hadn't said the wrong thing, that I hadn't ruined things. "You want to do the test?"

He nodded.

"I'll call Maggie."

His fingers weaved into my hair, holding me against him. "Later," he whispered, fingers stroking down my throat. "For now, I just need to hold the woman I love."

And that was when I learned that care came in many more forms than I'd first expected.

It could be a hug.

It could a fierce reply to snap someone out of a despairing mood.

It could be gentle touches.

It could be . . . me holding this man under the moonlight, knowing that, as unfeasible as it might seem, he had found a slice of heaven in my arms.

No strings. No rules. No barriers. Just love driving my every action, Talbot in my heart . . .

And I knew that I wouldn't go wrong so long as I kept him there.

CHAPTER TWENTY-FIVE

Talbot

I GOT the results just after I had lost my sword in a big battle and been captured by the enemies. The director called cut, and we all began to go our separate ways for the evening.

The P.A. came over with my cell in her hand. "Tammy's on the line."

Taking it with a thanks, I stepped away from everyone and headed toward my trailer. I was covered with fake blood and grime, had a simulated cut on my cheek and one down my forearm. My shirt was in tatters, my chain mail having already been removed by the costume crew, and I was holding my breath as I listened to Tammy say hello on the other end of the line.

"Hi, baby," she said.

"How was your day?" I asked.

"No escapades with the Milk Caper, if that's what you're asking. How was yours? Your knight get all the baddies yet?"

"Unfortunately not." A beat. "I miss you."

She was back in Utah, had left on my plane with me, the pilot making a pit stop to drop her at a private airport outside of Darlington, while I'd flown on to England.

We'd been together three weeks, and I missed her like we'd been together for three years. Missed her even more when she did things like she was doing right now—a quiet sigh, her tone soft. "Tal," she said, before her voice returned to its normal crisp tenor. "None of that. We promised."

"You badgered," I pointed out. "I finally just gave in."

"And you've discovered the reason our relationship is working."

I laughed. "You're perfect for me?"

"Damned right, I am," she said, with a laugh, but her voice was all soft and sweet, mirroring the way I loved her. Okay, that was a lie, because I loved her any which way, but most especially when she went back to her commanding, police officer tone and added, "I have the night shift tonight, so I need to tell you—"

And that was when I knew.

"He's my father, isn't he?"

A moment of silence.

Then a barely audible, "Yes. I'm sorry to say, he is."

I hadn't made it back to my trailer, and the news had my feet freezing for several long moments.

"Tal?" she asked.

I unstuck, kept walking until I made it back to the white vehicle, reaching for the door and tugging it open but not stepping inside. "I'm here," I said. "I'm . . . not okay exactly." But I realized now that some part of me must have known that was who the man was from the moment Maggie had called, a little more than ten days ago now.

"Do you need me to fly over?"

She would, too.

I knew that without a doubt.

"No," I said. "I have some stuff to sort out, starting with why he'd want to hurt me, but . . . I'm going to put it aside for now and just focus on the now. On us. On the film." And not why my father had shown up with all that rage, why he'd come after all these years, how he'd known where I lived—though I supposed the last wasn't too difficult considering the mob I'd had outside my gate. "I just . . . I guess part of me had already accepted that it was likely, and now . . ."

"You have the answer, but not the why. The toxicology report shows numerous substances," she said gently. "So, that's probably a big part of the why."

That was true, especially since it was a big part of the *why* of my childhood.

Drugs, and how they could devastate a family.

"Yeah," I whispered, finally stepping inside.

"You sure you don't want me to come over?" she asked. "I'm sure Rob would give me some more time off."

"No, sweetheart. I'll be okay." A beat as I closed the door behind me. "I'll call you if things get dicey and—"

"You'd better."

I looked up.

Because that voice had registered both through my phone and also through the . . . air. Tammy was standing in my trailer, smudges beneath her eyes, a backpack at her feet, and the softest, gentlest smile on her lips. My cell ended up on the couch. She ended up in my arms.

"What are you doing here?"

Her fingers brushed my jaw. "I'm here because I care."

My heart thudded, and I hugged her tighter. "*God,* I love you."

Lips on my cheek, hands in my hair. "I love you, even though I'm now covered with fake blood and dirt."

"Shit." I pulled back so that her gray sweatshirt was stained with smudges of brown and smears of red. "I'm sorry."

Her fingers trailed down my chest, through the tatters of my costume shirt. "Although," she murmured, "I do have to say that I don't mind this look too much, even if it is a little messy." She stepped close again.

"Wait." I caught her wrists, not wanting to get her any dirtier than she already was.

"No, I don't think I *will* wait." Her arms came around my neck, her front pressed to mine, and I groaned at the feel of her breasts on my naked chest, even with the layers of fabric between us. "You know the best part about you in this role?"

"What's that?" I managed, even though I was having a very hard time concentrating with her hips undulating against mine.

"You being all dirty," she murmured, rising on tiptoe and her lips finding mine, "and you getting *me* all dirty means that we get to wash it off." A brush of her mouth. "Together."

"Together?" I asked.

"Yup." She glanced over my shoulder. "I'm guessing you have a shower in here?"

"It's tiny."

Her smile turned wicked. "Well, even luckier for us."

That wicked grin snapped the last thread of my control. I scooped her up, carried her to the bathroom and made quick work of removing our clothes. A few moments later, we were in the shower—or attempting to, anyway.

Because it *was* truly tiny.

And try as we might, two grown-ass adults couldn't properly fit.

One of us always had an arm or leg out the top or side, and it was a struggle to stay warm and not flood the bathroom, let alone wash ourselves.

But then with some sheer determination on Tammy's part, she managed to get us clean enough that we could stumble out, use towels to wipe up most of the water, make our way to the bed, and flop down. We were both laughing so hard that it was impossible to do anything but cling to each other and wait until we'd found some semblance of control.

Eventually, I managed, rolling her to her back, holding those gorgeous hazel eyes in my gaze. "Thank you," I murmured.

Her hands cupped my face. "I love you."

"You're my heart."

The smile she gave me patched over all those empty spots, filled me with so much joy and hope that I didn't care about my father and all the answers I didn't—and probably would never —have.

My childhood had been a mess. My parents hadn't been good.

Those were facts.

But I had something more now.

I had Tammy and Maggie and Aaron, Eden, Pierce, and Artie. I was building a family that was my own, one that was healthy, that I could rely on.

And whatever happened with the man who'd fathered me wouldn't change any of that.

Because my family had my back.

And while the giant gaping holes inside me weren't completely gone, they were getting smaller, filling in, and I knew that eventually they might disappear altogether.

Until then?

Tammy's lips found mine.

I had this, had *her*.

And that was so much more than enough.

EPILOGUE

Talbot, Six Months Later

"WE DON'T HAVE to do this," I said when I felt Tammy trembling next to me.

We were standing backstage, listening to the rumble of voices just beyond the curtain of the daytime talk show that saw millions of viewers a day. It was the feel-good capital of the world, the one telling everyone to be kind to each other, and it was the perfect place to get the real story out.

It was also part of Maggie's plan.

Tammy swallowed hard, looking fucking beautiful in the slacks and button-down that she'd picked out from the rack of clothes Maggie had brought by the house that morning. Her hair was down, flowing in a shining sheet beyond her shoulders, and the makeup people had made her approach supermodel beauty.

She'd probably say I was biased.

And I supposed I was.

She was fucking gorgeous made up like this, and also amazingly beautiful with her hair pulled back, nothing on her face.

I was whipped.

After six months. Well, it had really only taken a few days before I'd gotten to that state. Okay, no, I suppose I'd been lost for her from the moment she'd started stripping down in front of me in that tiny, walled garden. Regardless of the exact timing of this woman stealing my heart, these last months had been the best of my life. As the cliché went, I fell more in love with Tammy every day, and life was smooth and easy and peaceful, especially since we spent the vast majority of our time in Darlington.

Now, however, with her terrified and looking pale enough to topple over, I took her hand, started tugging her back toward the green room.

We didn't need to do this.

It took a few moments before she realized what was happening.

"What are you doing?" she said, dragging her heels, scrabbling at my hold.

"You're terrified. You don't want to do this." I wrapped my fingers around her wrist when she slipped free. "So, you're not doing this."

"I'm fine," Tammy said, breaking my hold. "I told you, I *want* to do this."

"*I'll* go out and talk to everyone."

She lifted her chin. "It's my charity," she said, moving beyond the bemused production assistants in the hall. "So, *I'm* the one talking about it."

"Tam—"

A girl with a clipboard stepped forward. "We're ready for you both."

I lifted a finger, took Tammy's hand again. "Just a second."

"Of course, Mr. Green."

"Tammy," I began, leaning over to whisper in her ear.

"I love you," she whispered, "but if you don't let me do this, so help me God, I will make you play *Munchkin* with me." A beat. "Twice."

I shuddered, not because the game was bad. It was actually really fun—except when someone was playing against Tammy, who took absolutely no quarter and destroyed me every single time.

It was on our banned games list.

Along with *Uno* because of my tactics—since I was a master with the Skip and Draw Four cards.

I looked forward to adding to the list, because it would mean more time together, more memories and moments with our family and friends and just each other. But right now, I didn't want Tammy to do something she didn't want to do.

"I'm just—"

"Looking out for me," she whispered. "I know, baby. But I *need* to do this."

"Mr. Green?" came a tentative voice, more urgent now.

Tammy took my hand this time and led me to the stage entrance. "We're ready," she said.

A moment later, the music blared, and we walked out to greet the host, to wave at the cheering audience, to talk about our relationship and my movies, and, most importantly, to tell everyone about the charity that Tammy had started.

WorldCare.

Whose first goal of operation was to connect kids with caring adults. Next would be the isolated elderly.

Such a simple concept, and so perfectly encapsulating this woman.

Later that week, when we were back in Darlington, cuddled on the couch as we watched the show air, and WorldCare's website crashed from all the donations, Tammy glanced at me with tears in her eyes and just whispered my favorite phrase of all time, "I love you."

And I'd be damned if I could find any holes inside me.

———

Hate missing Elise's new releases? Love contests, exclusive excerpts and giveaways?

Then signup for Elise's newsletter here!

http://eepurl.com/bdnmEj

———

LOVE, CAMERA, ACTION

Dotted Line

Action Shot

Close Up

End Scene

Meet Cute

LOVE, CAMERA, ACTION

Did you miss any of the other Love, Camera, Action series books? Check out excerpts from the series below or find the full series at http://elisefaber.com/LoveCameraAction

———

Dotted Line
Love, Camera, Action #1
Get your copy at books2read.com/DottedLine

Olivia

THE COLD VOICE hit my spine before I made it to my chair.

"What did you say?"

Cole McTavish.

A tall hunk of a former hockey player, all muscled thighs and towering height, with a face that would have been classified as beautiful if not for the several-times-broken nose, the jagged scar along his jaw, and the small, smooth one bisecting his left eyebrow.

Further that, he was about as opposite from me as anyone

I'd ever met.

Relaxed, always ready with an easy smile, Cole never raised his voice—at least *off* the ice. On it, he'd been a terror, a virtually unstoppable force who'd fought when needed and didn't back down from protecting a teammate.

I'd also been his agent while he was playing.

After he'd retired, I'd transitioned him over to Devon, who'd helped him refine his brand for post-playing opportunities. Now, he was the face for a few hockey companies and one well-known corporation that sold watches. Though, to my and the rest of the female populace's dismay, he'd turned down the swimwear ads.

I'd been with him in the locker room enough to know what was under those flannel shirts and jeans.

It was definitely billboard worthy.

Lane started to push by him, but Cole grabbed his shoulder and stepped into my office, forcing Lane back.

Devon Scott trailed them in, a stormy expression on his face.

I glanced at my boss and shook my head, silently telling him I'd already handled it, but Dev shook his head firmly back at me. Which was when I realized that what Lane had said must have been worse than I'd thought. Normally, Devon would never get involved in an argument between my employees and myself unless I asked him to.

Which I didn't.

Since I handled my own shit.

"Tell her what you said."

My gaze flashed to Cole and his darkened face. "It's—"

Emerald eyes locked onto mine, sparking fire. "Tell her," he said, and Lane must have realized exactly how deep of a pile of shit he'd dived into because when I broke Cole's stare to glance at my assistant, his face had gone pale.

I rested my hip against my desk. "I don't need to hear it. Lane, get the file."

Devon crossed his arms. "Tell her," he said. "If you're man

enough to mutter it under your breath, you're man enough to say it aloud."

Lane shook off Cole and spun to face me. "Fine," he snapped. "I said that you're such a fucking bitch."

My lips curved and I huffed. "Okay, great, thanks. Now, back to work."

Lane's jaw fell open.

A curl of amusement crept onto Dev's face.

Cole appeared even more infuriated.

Lane somehow went paler. "Wh-what?"

"I've got a ton of work," I told him, "and you say bitch like it's a bad thing." I transferred my gaze to Cole and Dev. "*All* of you are acting like it's the worst insult in the world." I laughed. "Believe me, I've been called worse."

"It's unacceptable," Dev said, and I loved the guy for it.

But this was also the way of the world.

Most men despised strong women. We were told to smile or look happy or be fine with the scraps they tossed our way. If I'd had an issue with men calling me a bitch, I would have quit this male-dominated field ten years ago when I'd been a lowly assistant like Lane and my boss had been a lot worse than a bitch.

But I hadn't.

I'd put my head down, got my shit done.

And I'd learned to not give two craps when a man thought I was a bitch.

Because it had become my anthem.

When I negotiated my client to have equivalent perks in their contract, I was a bitch.

When I demanded a different client have access to the same off-season training as the rest of the team, I was a bitch.

When I secured a bonus that was similar to the rest of the big names on the roster, I was a bitch.

So, fine.

I was a bitch.

Great. Congrats. Moving on.

—Get your copy at www.books2read.com/DottedLine

———

Action Shot

Love, Camera, Action #2

Get your copy at books2read.com/ActionShot

Artie

"A lady doesn't give away her secrets."

Stormy gray-blue eyes went hot. "I bet I can convince you."

My pussy clenched. Straight up, right then. With a single look. *Uh-oh.* "I don't date children."

He laughed. "I'm twenty-two. That's hardly a child."

"Pierce. I'm thirty-seven."

"So?"

He meant it, too, I could tell.

"So, I don't date people who work with me."

His laughter burned a hole straight down to my middle. "I think we've quite established the fact that we're not going to be working together."

He had a point. And the stink knew it, given the way those hot eyes traced me up and down.

"Eat your pasta," he ordered huskily. Normally orders from men pissed me off, especially men who were many years younger than me, who deigned to think they had a right to give me orders, but there was something about Pierce's gaze, heavy with approval and desire, that made it less annoying and more . . . promising.

I lifted a brow. "And if I don't?"

"I'll just have to—" He broke off and waggled his brows, making like he was going to grab my plate.

I lifted my fork threateningly.

He laughed, went back to his own entrée. "Thanks for lunch."

My carefully constructed bite of pasta fell onto my plate. "I thought we'd established *you* were paying," I said and when he did nothing more but chuckle and then smolder at me again, before continuing to devour his lunch, I knew I was in trouble.

Then deep shit when he snagged the waiter and handed him his card.

And then falling down into a crevice of even deeper shit when he gently tugged my ponytail out from underneath the collar of my jacket when I slipped it on.

Between the table and front door, I considered my options.

At the front door, I made a decision.

I took his hand and pulled him over to my car.

—Get your copy at www.books2read.com/ActionShot

———

Close Up
Love, Camera, Action #3
www.books2read.com/Closeupef

Eden

Smiling to myself, I reached into my purse for my keys then promptly dropped them to the ground.

Ugh.

I bent—

"I know that ass."

A gasp of outrage on my lips, I straightened and whipped around, ready to tell off the arrogant bastard who'd dared—

Damon Garcia.

Photographer extraordinaire and—

He grinned.

Man who still wanted to get into my pants.

Now, I wasn't a prude. I slept around enough to have been called a whore by more than one publication. It wasn't like my activities between the sheets were more than most men in Hollywood, but because I was a woman, it was noticed and frowned upon.

I just couldn't bring myself to care.

I practiced consensual, safe sex.

If we both were attracted to each other and it was safe, then I didn't hesitate to go for what I wanted.

Maybe that made me a whore.

Maybe I didn't care what other people thought about me.

But Damon?

Damon, I didn't sleep with.

Damon, I didn't fuck or kiss or touch.

Because I knew if I allowed myself a taste, I would never have enough.

I was frozen in place when he bent in front of me and picked up my keys, extending them toward me. That was when I made my first mistake. My fingers brushed his as I took them back. Heat exploded up my arm, my stomach went tingly, and my voice was breathy as I asked, "What are you doing here?"

"I live here now. Well, not the hospital—I'm visiting a friend —but here in town." He smiled, and that paired with the news of him being in L.A. hit me hard upside the head. So hard, it knocked my common sense loose and allowed me to make my second mistake.

Because I didn't run after I'd said, "Oh, that's great."

My third came when he asked, "Want to grab a drink tonight and catch up?"

To which I said, "Yes," instead of "Absolutely not."

My fourth?

Well, my fourth came when I finally gave in to the draw that was Damon Garcia and woke up naked in my bed beside him.

And then he wouldn't leave.

—Get your copy at www.books2read.com/Closeupef

———

End Scene
Love, Camera, Action #4
www.books2read.com / EndScene

MY CELL VIBRATED JUST as the minister declared, "You may now kiss the bride."

Slipping out of my chair as Eden and Damon locked lips, but before they vacated the altar, I sprinted down the aisle and toward a tree, hustling behind it.

Only five people were currently *not* on Do Not Disturb.

Eden—who was currently otherwise occupied.

Three additional equally important clients. All of whom were either in attendance—and Pierce and Artie were not likely to be on the phone as they watched the bride and groom get hitched—or on the opposite side of the globe—and Talbot was probably sleeping.

The last was my father.

Who *never* called unless something was on fire, someone was bleeding out, or an asteroid was heading toward the planet.

I glanced at the screen, not realizing how much I'd been hoping it was Talbot with some earth-shattering crisis until I saw "Dad calling" flashing across the surface. "Shit," I muttered, swiping a finger and bringing it up to my ear. "Hi, Dad. Everything okay?"

"It's not Dad."

Hot then cold. Goose bumps on my arms. The past shoving its way firmly into my present because his voice was ice, and it broke my heart.

Aaron.

My *ex* Aaron.

My ex because I'*d* left.

—Get your copy at www.books2read.com / EndScene

ALSO BY ELISE FABER

Crashed (July 27th, 2021)

Breakers Hockey (all stand alone)
Broken (May 24th, 2021)

KTS Series
Fire and Ice (Hurt Anthology, stand alone)
Riding The Edge
Crossing The Line (March 22nd, 2021)
Leveling The Field (June 14th, 2021)

Love, Action, Camera (all stand alone)
Dotted Line
Action Shot
Close-Up
End Scene
Meet Cute (April 5th, 2021)

Love After Midnight (all stand alone)
Rum And Notes
Virgin Daiquiri
On The Rocks
Sex On The Seats (April 26th, 2021)

Life Sucks Series (all stand alone)
Train Wreck
Hot Mess
Dumpster Fire
Clusterf*@k (August 16th, 2021)

Roosevelt Ranch Series (all stand alone, series complete)
Disaster at Roosevelt Ranch

Heartbreak at Roosevelt Ranch

Collision at Roosevelt Ranch

Regret at Roosevelt Ranch

Desire at Roosevelt Ranch

Phoenix Series **(read in order)**

Phoenix Rising

Dark Phoenix

Phoenix Freed

Phoenix: LexTal Chronicles **(rereleasing soon, stand alone, Phoenix world)**

From Ashes

In Flames

To Smoke (October 18th, 2021)

Stand Alones

Someday, Maybe (YA)

ABOUT THE AUTHOR

USA Today bestselling author, Elise Faber, loves chocolate, Star Wars, Harry Potter, and hockey (the order depending on the day and how well her team -- the Sharks! -- are playing). She and her husband also play as much hockey as they can squeeze into their schedules, so much so that their typical date night is spent on the ice. Elise changes her hair color more often than some people change their socks, loves sparkly things, and is the mom to two exuberant boys. She lives in Northern California. Connect with her in her Facebook group, the Fabinators or find more information about her books at www.elisefaber.com.

facebook.com/elisefaberauthor

amazon.com/author/elisefaber

bookbub.com/profile/elise-faber

instagram.com/elisefaber

goodreads.com/elisefaber

pinterest.com/elisefaberwrite